# A WALK IN THE SUN

Recent  *Borzoi Novels*

# *THIS  WAR:*

### ITALY

*One Man's War*
Sgt. Charles E. (Commando) Kelly
with Pete Martin

### RUSSIA

*The Tempering of Russia*    Ilya Ehrenburg

### SICILY

*A Bell for Adano*    John Hersey

### NORTH AFRICA

*Desert Conquest*    Russell Hill

### FRANCE

*Army of Shadows*    Joseph Kessel

### GUADALCANAL

*Into the Valley*    John Hersey

### BURMA, CHINA, INDIA

*They Shall Not Sleep*    Leland Stowe

PUBLISHED BY ALFRED A. KNOPF

# A WALK
# IN THE SUN

BY *Harry Brown*

NEW YORK

ALFRED · A · KNOPF

1 9 4 4

# A WALK IN THE SUN

# I

THE LIEUTENANT had been wounded while they were still on the water. He was a slight, dark man named Rand, rather silly, and if he hadn't been doing something silly at the time he might never have been wounded. He had taken out his glasses and was leaning against the side of the landing barge, trying to focus on some firing off to the left. It was the first of the firing. Evidently one of the shore batteries had decided something was wrong and they had sent over a couple of shells. One of the destroyers had replied, a cruiser had joined in, and some batteries farther along the coast had also opened up. No one was hitting anything, and the whole action was taking place about three miles away.

The gun flashes were spectacular, however, and Lieutenant Rand had taken out his field glasses to watch what was going on. Not that he could see anything. That was the silly part of it. He might have been able to pick up the silhouette of a destroyer for a second, but by the time he could have adjusted his glasses the destroyer would have zigzagged out of range. The destroyers weren't waiting around for the lieutenant. Nevertheless he stuck his head up in the air and tried to pick up one of the ships, or possibly one of the shore batteries. Of course, disregarding the fact that it was a pointless thing to do, there seemed to be no danger in it. The firing was some miles off, the barge was still about twenty-four hundred yards from shore, and the night, or rather early morning, was dark. There were no stars. And in a way it was a natural act on Lieutenant Rand's part. He was bored and he was nervous. He had been in the barge for some hours, and it was not the most comfortable place in the world. As the time of landing approached a growing tension was added to nervousness and discomfort. The men's mouths were dry. Sounds magnified themselves. The dark closed in like a smotherer's pillow.

Lieutenant Rand, a wry young man, had a dry natural curiosity, one that manifested itself in a love of facts. He had often expressed regret in mess that he was not in the artillery, because the computation of trajectory and like subjects fascinated him. Before the war he had been a C.P.A. in Hartford, Connecticut, and had he come a little later in the draft, or a little earlier, he might have found himself as a Finance officer in some quiet Army backwater. As things turned out, however he came just at the right time to be sent to the Infantry, and then to OCS, and then, much too hurriedly for his ordered mind, to the Mediterranean. He was new to the company, replacing Lieutenant Grimes, who had been picked off by a sniper while climbing a wall in a small town near Gela, in Sicily. The company had gone through the whole Si-

cilian campaign short an officer, until Lieutenant Rand
had finally caught up with it in Messina. This landing
operation was the first action he had ever seen, and
the guns that were flashing over on the left were the
first serious guns he had ever heard. Therefore, to
his logical mind it was logical that he watch them.

One of the shore batteries evidently decided that
there was a whole fleet behind the cruiser and the destroyer. Its fire moved aimlessly over the sea in the
direction of the barges, as though the shells were feeling for something. No one paid a great deal of attention to either the shells or Lieutenant Rand. As far
as the men were concerned the shells could take care
of themselves, and so could the lieutenant. When one
burst very near the barge the men took it without
rancor. They knew that the shells were disinterested;
they were not aimed for them. A man can always tell
when a shell is looking for him. A shell that is seeking
a man out doesn't whine. It snarls. So when the shell
struck near the barge some of the men said "Bastards,"
impersonally and quite without feeling, and let it go
at that. And when the next shell, almost immediately
afterwards, struck some three hundred yards to the
right, they knew that there was no need to worry.

Lieutenant Rand had his glasses to his eyes when
the shell struck, trying to adjust them with the thumb
and middle finger of his left hand. He had pushed his
helmet back on his head, because the steel rim kept
getting in the way of the eyepieces, and it annoyed
him. He was aware of a great mushrooming white-
ness in front of him, and then someone pinched his
left cheek very hard. Lieutenant Rand said "Oh,"

5

and turned around to see who was pinching him. Then he slid slowly down to a sitting position.

Sergeant Porter, who had been standing behind the lieutenant, felt a steady pressure on the calf of one leg. When he looked to find out what it was he could dimly make out the lieutenant sitting on the floor of the barge, his hands hanging down at his sides. At first he thought that Rand had gone to sleep, and for a moment he felt annoyed that he should choose to sleep when it was almost time to pile out. Then he remembered that a moment before Lieutenant Rand had been standing up looking over the side. A shell had hit quite close, too. No one could go to sleep that quickly, unless he'd been without sleep for days. Sergeant Porter bent down by the lieutenant.

"Anything the matter, sir?" he asked.

"Oh," Lieutenant Rand said. "Oh. Oh." The words were more a surprised grunt than anything else. The lieutenant did not move his arms.

Cautiously Sergeant Porter ran his hands over Rand's chest. He felt nothing. Then he touched his face.

"Jesus," he said. "All gone."

He wiped his hand on his thigh. "Pete," he said. "Hey, Pete."

Staff Sergeant Halverson came over. "What's the matter?"

"Shell splinter got the lieutenant. Smashed his face all to hell."

Halverson bent down. "I can't see anything," he said.

"I can feel it," Sergeant Porter said. "Messy. I think it took his whole face away."

"Where's your flashlight?"

"You can't shine a light out here, Pete."

"Oh. Oh," Lieutenant Rand said. He caught his breath twice.

"I can shine a light if I have to shine a light. Where's the thing?"

Porter took his flashlight out of the hip pocket of his fatigues and passed it to Halverson. "Cover over him," Halverson said. "I'm just going to take a quick look."

They bent over Rand, their helmets almost touching. Halverson switched on the light. "I told you," Sergeant Porter said. Lieutenant Rand's left cheek and eye were covered with blood. It was impossible to make out whether or not the eye was still there. Even by the brief, dim glare of the flashlight the two sergeants could see that a good part of his cheek had been carried away. Jagged white bits of bone, splinters from a smashed zygoma, stuck out at several places. Blood dripped down on his shoulder. Lieutenant Rand's mouth kept opening and closing, like the gills of a fish out of water. His good eye was wide open.

"Douse that light," somebody hissed.

Staff Sergeant Halverson switched off the flashlight. "Go get that god-damned First Aid man. What's his name? McWilliams. He might as well start earning his money."

"Where is he?" Porter asked.

"Down in the stern," Halverson said. "I saw him down in the stern."

Porter picked his way among the men towards the stern. The night was so dark that men five yards away from the lieutenant did not know he had been wounded. There was a silent cluster of cramped figures in the stern. "Where's McWilliams?" Porter said. "Where's McWilliams, the First Aid man?"

"Who's that?" a man said.

"Sergeant Porter."

One of the figures rose to his feet and broke with the darkness. "Here I am, Sergeant," McWilliams said. "You want me?"

"The lieutenant's hurt up front," Porter said. "Sergeant Halverson said for you to go up."

"What's the matter with him, Sergeant?" McWilliams wanted to know. He spoke in a slow, dispassionate drawl.

"Get the hell up and see," Porter said. "You want me to bring him down here?"

"I was just asking," said McWilliams. He moved toward the front of the barge.

"What's the matter with the lieutenant, Sergeant?" a man asked. "Old rockin' chair get him?" Porter recognized the voice as that of Rivera, a machine-gunner.

"God-damn shell got him," he said.

Rivera whistled. "No kidding?" a man said. "Honest to God?" said another. "That's the trouble with these tubs," Rivera said. "They only make the armor plate six inches thick. That wouldn't keep out a BB from a BB Daisy air gun. You mean that one that hit so close?"

Porter nodded his head wearily, then remembered

that no one could see him nodding in the dark. "Yeah," he said.

"He dead?" Rivera asked.

"Not yet," Sergeant Porter said. "He had his head over the side. He was looking through the binoculars."

"That's a Purple Heart, sure as hell," Rivera said. "How'd you like to have a Purple Heart, Jakie?"

"Depends where I got the Purple Heart," Private Friedman said. "In the leg, okay. In the guts, no."

"A Purple Heart means a nice quiet trip to Jersey City," Rivera said. "I would like a nice quiet trip to Jersey City."

"I'd like a nice quiet trip anywheres," said Private Judson. "I ain't had a quiet trip since this war started. Jersey City will do fine."

"It blew the hell out of the side of his head," Sergeant Porter said. He felt guilty, as though Lieutenant Rand's wound was a secret that he shouldn't be telling. He knew he should go back and see if there was anything he could do, but he did not want to go back. He did not want to help Halverson. If the lieutenant was going to die, he was going to die, and there was nothing Eddie Porter could do about it. Nothing in the world.

"In the head, no," Private Friedman said. "I don't want a Purple Heart in the head."

"Joey Sims got a Purple Heart in the head," Rivera said. "I bet to Christ he'll look better when they're through with him than you do now."

"It depends on the position," Private Friedman said. "Position is everything in life."

"Is Sergeant Halverson in command now, Sergeant?" Rivera asked.

"He knows what to do," Porter said. Halverson had been in command before, after they lost Lieutenant Grimes. Halverson had been in command almost from Gela all the way to Messina. Halverson had done all right. If the captain had liked him a little more, he probably would have been commissioned in the field. But the captain had preferred to hang on and wait for a replacement. The platoon had had very bad luck with lieutenants. First Grimes, and now Rand. If Halverson had got the breaks he might have been sitting very pretty right now.

Porter was just as glad that Halverson hadn't got the breaks, for Porter did not like Halverson. He was afraid of him. Halverson was cold and competent, and Porter distrusted coldness and competence. Even in a war, he felt, the human element should enter in. He did not, of course, think of it just in that way, nor could he have phrased it in such a fashion if he had been called upon to do so. There was enough coldness and competence in the machines, the tanks and the planes. Nothing was colder than a battened-down tank moving over a field. It was cold, heartless, brainless, but it was alive. It could reason and it could kill. Sergeant Porter was afraid of tanks in the same way he was afraid of Sergeant Halverson. Sergeant Porter was not a good soldier, not because he was afraid, but because he was afraid of the wrong things. All soldiers, unless they have gone berserk, are afraid, but there are qualities and grades of fear. There is more to war than the rifle and the knife thrust in the dark.

The knot of men lapsed into silence in the darkness. They really had not wanted to talk, but they had forced themselves to say something. Talking was a form of bravado. If a man said something, no matter what it was, it seemed to him that he was saying: "Here I am, very calm, very collected. Nothing's going to happen to me. The rest of the company's going to be wiped out, but nothing's going to happen to me. See, I can talk. I can form sentences. Do you think I could make conversation if I knew I was going to die?" Yet every man, inwardly, had a hard core of doubt that rested in the pit of his stomach and threatened to disgorge itself at any moment. Their voices, when they talked, were strange, but none of them noticed the strangeness, because when each man spoke his own voice sounded odd, and so it all seemed correct somehow. If a phonograph record of the men's voices had been made then and played back to them later, not one of them would have recognized himself. They would have thought it was a joke—a very elaborate joke. And in a way it would have been.

Sergeant Porter worked his way back toward the bow of the barge. Once he stepped on a man's hand, and the man swore at him. Porter paid no attention.

Three or four of the platoon were gathered around Lieutenant Rand. Halverson was leaning against the side of the barge. In the darkness McWilliams was sprinkling sulfa on the wound. "How is he?" Porter asked. Halverson shrugged in the dark. "He's stopped his noise," he said. "I thought he was going to say something a while back. He tried to say something. Where were you?"

"Down there," Porter said.

"I wanted you."

"What for?"

"It doesn't matter now," Halverson said. "Stick around."

"You going to take over?" Sergeant Porter asked.

"I've got to see the captain," Halverson said. "As soon as we land I've got to see him. That is, if I can find him. I can't take over without seeing him."

Porter tried to make out Halverson's expression, but all he could see was shadows. He knew that Halverson was looking at him, and the thought made him frown, made him want to say something. He didn't like to have people looking at him. It made him nervous. It always had.

"Do you know what to do?" he asked.

"There's a house," Halverson said. "A farm. Three or four houses, as a matter of fact. That's where we're going."

"Pretty hard to find, isn't it?"

"That's the objective. It's on the map. There's a road from the beach leads right past it."

"How far?"

"A hell of a way. Six miles."

The frown deepened on Porter's face. "What the hell do they expect on the beach, a reception committee?" he said.

"That's the story," Halverson said. "That's all I know. How's it coming, Mac?"

"All right, I guess," McWilliams said. "We better get him to a doctor, though, or he ain't going to be pretty any more. He might not be alive any more, either."

"Bad, hey?" Halverson said.

"I guess so," McWilliams said. "I guess he got a pretty bad shock, too. He's trying to talk all the time. Can't you hear him?"

The two sergeants listened. "I don't hear anything," Porter said.

"It ain't words," McWilliams said. "It's just talk."

"Where are his binoculars?" Halverson wanted to know.

"They must have fallen overboard," Porter said. "I didn't hear them fall."

Halverson bent down. "Is he comfortable, Mac?"

"He wouldn't know whether he was comfortable or not," McWilliams said. "No sense in moving him, though. He'll be all right where he is."

"That's good," Halverson said. He rose to his feet. "Hell of a thing."

"He don't mind," said McWilliams.

The whole barge knew that the lieutenant had been wounded, but no one seemed terribly interested. It was not that they didn't care. It was simply that most of them had seen a lot of death, and death, unless it was of a really special variety, was not something that a man got up and moved around to investigate. There was no sense in getting up and walking over just to see a wounded man, even if you knew him quite well. And besides, the lieutenant was new. He hadn't been with the company more than—how long was it?—oh, two weeks or so. Not really long enough to get acquainted, anyway. He hadn't really slugged it out in the field with them. He didn't know anything about the Kasserine or Bizerte or any of those places. He was, as a matter of fact, a visitor who had come to stay a little while and then had gone away. The company wouldn't ever see him again, in all probability, nor would his platoon, which probably knew him better than anyone else. After all, he was lucky. It was quick in and quick out for Lieutenant Rand.

"What did the lieutenant do before he got in the Army?" Private Archimbeau asked. Not that he really cared. He just wanted to make conversation. He wanted to talk.

"He was a civilian," Private Trasker said. "A lousy civilian."

"You kill me," Private Archimbeau said.

"He was a business man," said Private Cousins. "He worked in an office."

"I worked in an office," Private Trasker said. "But I wasn't no business man."

"The whole god-damned army's made up of business men," said an unidentified voice.

"You kill me," said Private Archimbeau. "He'll be a business man in 1958, when we're fighting the Battle of Tibet. I got the facts down cold. They'll put him on a nice hospital ship and take him to a nice hospital and give him a couple of medals and take him home and give him his walking papers. Then he'll go back to business while we fight the Battle of Tibet. I got the facts."

"Maybe he'll die," Private Cousins said.

"Nobody dies," said Private Trasker.

The lieutenant's wound worried Corporal Tyne. Not that Rand was a good man or anything like that; not at all. Rand, as far as Corporal Tyne knew, wasn't a very good man at all. Competent, maybe—but not good. In the Army the word "good" is a superlative. A good officer is the Merriwell type. He always gets where he wants to go, and he keeps his casualties down. He knows when to be hard and when to relax. He will bear down on his men in barracks, but when he's out in the field he will call them Joe and Charlie and swear at them and pat them on the back as though he were the coach of a football team. Lieutenant Rand had never called any of his men Joe or Charlie, nor had he sworn at them or patted them on the back. He had taken them as they came, rather like figures on an adding machine, and he had always seemed slightly surprised that they added up to human beings. Rand was a quiet, aloof man who had a habit of doing the wrong thing quietly and aloofly. He hadn't really been at home in the Infantry, even in the little time he had been with the company. You had to be calm, and Rand wasn't calm, even though he walked measuredly and never smiled and ate with a solemn, rather annoying preciseness. If Rand had been a calm man he would never have stuck his head over the side of the barge and tried to make out the firing.

But he had, and there he was, sitting down and gasping, his cheek torn to shreds. That put it on Halverson again. Tyne absent-mindedly pushed his helmet, the straps of which hung loosely on either side of his face, down hard. It gave him a warm, comfortable feeling. Halverson would be all right. He knew his way around. He had done a nice job in Sicily, keeping his eyes open, doing the right thing, never getting out of line. Corporal Tyne admired Halverson; he didn't like him, but he admired him. For what he did, he was a good man.

"You should have seen his face." It was Sergeant Porter.

"I've seen faces before," Tyne said.

"Yeah, but the first time, before anything had happened. The guy may die, Bill."

Corporal Tyne said nothing. He studied Sergeant Porter's figure, looming before him. Porter was a good three inches taller than he was, and heavier. Fatter, too. His face, had Tyne been able to see it, would have been a cross between a thug's and a child's. Sergeant Porter's eyes always looked just a little frightened, but he had the heavy jaw of a preliminary boy. He was a beautiful drill sergeant, but he seemed to lack something in the field. Two hundred years ago, when battles had been parades, Eddie Porter would have done all right, but not now. He could not quite seem to connect the facts of battle in his mind, did not seem to realize that men no longer marched into machine-guns, that they went in or, better, around them on their bellies, hugging every blade of grass or pebble that would give them a bit of cover. It was amazing how big a blade of grass could seem when the bullets were cutting over one's head. Sergeant Porter didn't understand that. Sergeant Porter, Tyne felt, did not comprehend war; it had passed him by and gone over his head, the way the bullets had. He did not comprehend it, and he was afraid of it.

"Halverson's taking over again," Sergeant Porter said.

"I thought so."

"I don't like it. We don't know where we're going. Halverson only has a vague idea of where we're going. Some farmhouse, that's all he knows. Some farmhouse six miles up a road. He doesn't know what's there or why. Probably the beach is mined."

"There shouldn't be any mines up here," Tyne said. "It should be like getting out of bed."

Porter felt in his pockets, searching for nothing. Through one pocket he scratched his thigh gently.

"He's got to see the captain," he said, "before he takes over. No one knows where the captain is. He might be in any god-damned barge on the ocean. They can't keep formation in the dark. I'm nervous, Bill."

"So am I. So's everybody. He'll find the captain, all right."

Corporal Tyne looked at the illuminated dial on his watch. "Nearly time," he said.

The lieutenant had stopped trying to talk, and his head had sunk down. "Stay with him, Mac," Staff Sergeant Halverson said. "You can pick us up later. When it gets light you'll see a road running from the beach. We'll be up that road."

"Can't we leave him here?" McWilliams asked. "I might get lost. I don't want to go walking around by myself up any damned road."

"Stay with him," said Halverson.

"I wish to God those guns would stop," McWilliams said.

Sergeant Halverson looked at his watch. Nearly

time. He started to work his way toward the stern of the boat. "Hoist tail," he said, over and over again. "Hoist tail." The barge perceptibly slackened speed. The men began to get to their feet. A few of them attempted to stretch. "Porter," Halverson called softly. "Where the hell are you, Porter?" "Here I am," Porter said. He moved toward the sound of Halverson's voice. Tyne followed him. "Listen, Porter," Halverson said. "Take them a hundred yards up from the barge and hit the dirt. I'll go find the captain and then come back. That's all you have to do. Take them up a hundred yards and then hit dirt. It doesn't matter where you are. I don't care if it's in a pigpen."

"Okay, Hal," Porter said.

The platoon gathered around Halverson. "Most of you know that the lieutenant got wounded," he said, "and until I see the captain I'm taking over. You know what to do. Just go with Sergeant Porter and do what he tells you. Understand?"

There was a soft, almost inaudible murmuration of voices. Off to the left the naval guns and the shore batteries fell suddenly silent.

"Cold water," said Private Rivera. "Every time it's cold water. Son of a bitch."

"I'll take you in in a wheel chair," Private Friedman said. "You and your Purple Heart." He began to hum softly.

> *"My mama done tol' me,*
> *When I was in knee pants,*
> *My mama done tol' me,—*
> *'Son . . .'"*

"Bing Crosby," said Private Rivera.

"That's what they call me," Friedman said.

"I wish to Christ I was home in bed," said Private Judson.

Corporal Tyne went over to the lieutenant, unstrapped his map case, and threw it over his own shoulder. It was funny that no one had thought to do that. There was always something, some little thing. Tyne didn't know what was in the map case, but there must be something.

He looked out over the bow of the barge at the approaching land. It seemed very flat, very level, but far in the distance he could see hills. Light was beginning to appear over the crest of the hills. When he had been a small boy, at summer camp, Corporal Tyne, along with two hundred and fifty other boys, had had to take a dip in cold water before breakfast.

# 2

THEY GOT off the barges into water that was waist deep but surprisingly warm. They kept to one side of the barge so that Lieutenant Rand wouldn't be disturbed. Halverson was the first out, and Porter followed him. As he hit the water Porter gasped, and then he realized that it wasn't as cold as he had thought it was going to be, and that the gasp had been purely automatic. All up and down the beach there was a clank of steel on steel and the scurrying of men.

"I'm going to find the captain now," Halverson said. "Get 'em up there, won't you, Porter?"

"Sure thing," Porter said.

Halverson disappeared in the darkness off to the left, the water gurgling around his waist.

Tyne jumped down beside Porter. "Take up the rear, will you, Bill?" Porter said. "See they all get off. We'll take it in single file." He started wading toward shore. Archimbeau got off the barge and followed him, and one by one the men hit the water. Tyne, standing by the prow, counted them as they splashed down. Twenty-four. Twenty-five. "Last one in's a bastard," Rivera said as he hopped off. Fifty-two, counted Tyne. One missing. McWilliams. That was all right. "Watch him, Mac," he called into the barge, and then began wading toward shore himself.

The landing was going beautifully. Not a shot had been fired from the shore. Evidently the enemy had been caught cold; they thought it was a fleet moving up the coast. They *must* have thought that. But whatever they thought, they'd be sending the planes over pretty soon. Tyne hadn't heard a plane all night. As he walked up the beach away from the water, following Judson, the last man out, he listened to the sounds going on around him. Men were moving everywhere. He heard a sudden high-pitched laugh that was cut short almost as soon as it began. Somewhere two helmets struck each other.

The silence was bad, very bad. If there had been firing they would at least have known that men were around, but in the silence they could only guess and expect the worst. It might be an ambush, a trap. It might be anything. The enemy might be fifty miles away or they might be lying around the beachhead waiting, with grenades and artillery and flame-throwers and tanks and God only knew what else. If a machine-gun should start up, a man would know what to do. But a man could not fight a vacuum.

The beach was pebbly and rough. Twice Sergeant Porter tripped on stones, and once he almost fell headlong. He was walking fast, because he did not want to spend too much time on the beach, where anything might happen. He wanted to get a hundred yards up from the water and then hit the ground. He still believed that the beach was mined, and as he walked he clenched his teeth and held his hand very tightly around his carbine. He tripped on another stone. "Jesus," he said.

An average pace was thirty inches. That made a hundred yards about a hundred and twenty paces. He had figured it out back on the barge. It was hard to concentrate on the mines and the distance and everything else all at the same time. The rocks on the beach grew larger and then suddenly broke off, at a slight rise, into high grass. Porter saw the dim outline of a tree. He counted off pace 103, and he stuck his hand out in front of him, on the chance that a tree might suddenly rear before his face. At pace 120 he stopped. "We'll hold here," he said aloud, to no one in particular. "Hit the dirt." Archimbeau hit the dirt. As the men came up they fanned out to right and left and sat down.

When Tyne came up to Sergeant Porter the sergeant was still standing, with Sergeant Hoskins, of B Squad, beside him. "All here," Tyne said. "Good," said Porter. "Let's take it easy." The two sergeants and the corporal sat down.

"Well, I just conquered Italy," Private Rivera said to Private Friedman.

"You can have it," Private Friedman said. "You can have the whole country. I don't want any part of it."

"I ain't going to give you any part of it," said Rivera. "I found the god-damned place, and it's mine."

"It's yours," said Private Friedman.

"Cold," Private Judson said.

"It can't be cold. It's sunny Italy," said Rivera.

"You read the wrong book," Friedman said.

"I read the Soldier's Handbook," said Rivera. "It said this was sunny Italy. You calling the Soldier's Handbook a liar?"

"What page?" Friedman wanted to know.

"I forget the god-damned page."

"You always forget the god-damned page," Friedman said. "I wouldn't trust you with a popgun."

"You got to trust me with a popgun," said Private Rivera. "I'm a machine-gunner with a machine-gun."

"You ain't safe to live with," said Private Friedman.

Tyne wished he could have a cigarette, but the very thought of a cigarette made his mouth feel dry. He took out his canteen and wet his lips. "How long do you think Hal will take?" Sergeant Porter asked.

"Shouldn't be long," Sergeant Hoskins said. Hoskins was a tall, quiet man from Nashville. He was Old Army, and in his day he had been broken more than a dozen times for drunkenness and kindred sins. He took it all in his stride. He had the Soldier's Medal, picked up in 1939 when he had saved a nurse from drowning in a Georgia pool. He was a good soldier, and, had he been dependable, he would have been a good officer. Halverson liked him, but didn't trust him. In Sicily the platoon had been held up once for twenty minutes while Hoskins sampled the wares of a deserted wineshop.

"We'll never find that christly road," Porter said.

About a mile to the left a machine-gun opened up.

"There it goes," Porter said.

"We know where we are now, all right," said Hoskins.

Tenseness came to Tyne's face with the quickness of a smile. He could feel all the muscles from his forehead to his chin grow taut and then as suddenly relax. It was as though he had received a somehow painless slap in the face. He opened his mouth and caught his breath between his teeth. The palms of his hands were sweaty.

"Bet they get her in ten minutes," Hoskins drawled.

For no reason at all, Tyne smiled. The war had resolved itself into one machine-gun, firing off somewhere in the distance. That was the only enemy—one small machine-gun. Once it was silenced, everything would be over. Everything. And they weren't even in on it. They had been given the spectator's role. They could sit off to one side and listen while the war was being fought and won. Life was as easy as that.

Tyne suddenly felt intensely hungry, hungry for anything—an apple, a slice of bread, a sour plum, butter. "Where's the gun?" he asked.

Hoskins listened. "Down by the beach. I can't see a damned thing."

Slowly it was getting light, brightening over the foothills to the east. The sun that had burned down on New Guinea was working its way over the Middle East toward the Apennines. It was becoming light enough to make out faces and expressions, and hands. When Tyne looked at his hands he saw that they were very dirty. He could not understand this phenomenon of war. A man's hands never seemed to be clean, whether he touched anything or not. Always moist grime seemed to settle in his palms and between his fingers. War was a dirty business; it had a special dirt that went with it, as old warehouses have a finely sifted dust that gathers in all their dark and hidden corners. Possibly a criminologist used to defining types of dirt and types of dust could take a sample from an infantryman's fingernail, put it under his microscope, and identify it as from a soldier. Soldiers' faces, no matter where they are fighting, are always dirty, and the dirt is always the same color, no matter where it comes from. Perhaps the soldier's dirt is a natural camouflage, tending to make him blend with the landscape. Whatever it is, it is always with him.

"How long will it take Halverson?" Sergeant Porter asked. "It shouldn't take him more than a few minutes to find the captain. He must have been right around there somewhere."

"This is the Army, boy," said Hoskins. "Nothing ever happens when it should in the Army. You know that."

"There was no god-damned need for Rand to get hurt."

"He done it, anyway."

"What are you going to do if Halverson doesn't come back, Porter?" Tyne asked.

"How the hell do I know?" Porter said. "Halverson didn't really know himself. Maybe the lieutenant knew. If Halverson doesn't come back we might just as well stay here for all the good it will do us."

"They'll be sending the planes over pretty soon," said Hoskins.

"The hell with the planes," Porter said. "If they send the planes we'll move. If Halverson can't do something without running to the captain it doesn't mean that we've got to sit around here and get blown apart. If the planes come over we take a powder. The hell with Halverson."

"Take a powder where?" Tyne asked.

"Try and find that farmhouse," said Porter. He pulled a blade of grass from the ground and started to break the stem in sections about an inch long.

Tyne was lying on one elbow, his legs stretched out. Lieutenant Rand's map case was under him; his hip bone rested on it. For a moment he thought of telling Porter that he had it; then he changed his mind. There would be time enough for that. Halverson, with any luck at all, would show up in a few minutes.

Tyne was annoyed at Porter. The sergeant was always finding something that either surprised him very much or worried him very much, and this was one of Porter's worrying days. The thing was, events had a habit of going wrong on Porter's worrying days. It was almost as though, by sheer force of will, he badgered Fate into changing a predestined course and making his life miserable.

There was, however, no reason for Porter's worrying. If one excepted the lieutenant's wound, things had gone very well so far. The spot had been a good one for a landing, the enemy had obviously been surprised, and by the time he could rally for a counterattack it would probably be too late. It was a very good landing, and if nothing happened for the next two hours or so, it would all be over but the shouting.

In two hours they would be getting the tanks and the artillery off, and if the tanks were hot that day and if they worked fast they would have a bridgehead that was out of enemy artillery range by nightfall. Porter, as yet, had no real reason for worrying. No real reason at all.

It was very cold. It always is, just before dawn. And no matter if a man has been out all night, he is apt to begin to shiver when four o'clock in the morning comes around. Perhaps the heat of his body goes down. Whatever the reason, he feels cold the most severely at that time. His feet grow icy; he shivers; his teeth chatter. Nothing can warm him. A fire does no good. Eventually the cold passes, but even at nine o'clock in the morning, in the sun, he is still cold. The early morning is a little like death.

"Sergeant, I want a discharge," Private Archimbeau said. "I'm all fought out."

"Shut up," Porter said dispassionately. Archimbeau talked a lot, but he was a good man.

"In the last war," said Private Archimbeau, "they sent a guy to France. That was all there was to it, they just sent him to France. Then he went home. Simple. Real simple. That's a nice kind of a war to have around. But what do they do this time? Do they send you to France? No, they do not send you to France. They send you to Tunisia, and then they send you to Sicily, and they send you to Italy. God knows where they'll send you after that. Maybe we'll be in France next year. Around Christmas time, maybe. Then we work our way east. Yugoslavia. Greece. Turkey. No, not Turkey. All I know is, in 1958 we're going to fight the Battle of Tibet. I got the facts."

"Kill that," Porter said.

Archimbeau stretched out on his back with his hands clasped behind his head. His rifle lay crosswise on his stomach. "So I want a discharge. A honorable discharge. I've done my share of it. They next guy can pick up where I left off."

"You tell 'em, Jack," said Private Trasker.

"It's taking them a hell of a long time to shut that gun up," Hoskins said. "I don't know what they're doing down there."

"Maybe they can't find it," Porter said.

"If it gets a few of them in the guts they'll find it," Hoskins said. "They'll find it then, boy."

"This is a lovely way to fight a war," Private Trasker said. "Just lie down and listen. And they're paying us, too."

The machine-gun chattered away over on the left. It was firing in short bursts. Evidently they were trying to get around it, and the gunners were saving up until they saw someone move—until they saw a rifle or a face or a helmet in the grass. That was the way they did it. If the gunner kept his finger on her you knew he had either plenty to shoot at or that he was a very stupid gunner. Few of the Germans were stupid gunners. Sometimes the Italians kept firing just for the sake of the noise.

"That's a Jerry gun," Sergeant Hoskins said.

"You sure?" Porter asked. "I never could tell the damned things apart."

"Sure I'm sure. I bet I can even tell you the color of the guy's hair."

"I think I hear planes," Tyne said.

Everybody listened. It was growing brighter by the minute. Now the platoon could make out a grove of trees about two hundred yards ahead of them. They saw no movement anywhere. Between the bursts of the machine-gun they listened.

"I guess I was wrong," Tyne said. "I thought I heard them."

"They'll probably be ours, anyway," Porter said.

"They'd better be," said Trasker. "We got enough guys in the Air Force. Hey, Jack, you know my brother's in the Air Force?"

"Where in the Air Force?" Archimbeau wanted to know.

"My kid brother, for Christ's sake," said Trasker. "He's in the States. Scott Field, Illinois. You ever hear of Scott Field, Illinois?"

"I never even heard of Illinois," Archimbeau said. "I don't get around much any more."

There were three muffled explosions, and the machine-gun fell silent. "Told you," Hoskins said. "Eight minutes."

"It should of been you, Rivera," Friedman said. "Always it should of been you."

"It always is me," Rivera said.

As it grew lighter they discovered that they could see neither the beach nor the water. They were in a little hollow among a few scraggly trees, and there was a slight sandy rise between them and the ocean. Now that the machine-gun had stopped there seemed to be no life around them. The area was alive with troops, but for all they knew it might have been a desert island. There was nothing to tell them that there was anyone around—no firing, no shouting, no sound of motors. Nothing. The destroyer and the cruiser had stopped firing long ago; so had the shore batteries. As day came, slowly and almost unwillingly, a soft wind drew in from the sea and stirred the trees over their heads. The wind carried with it the smell of rain.

Inland the wood waited for them. Porter thought he saw a piece of road along one side of it, but he couldn't be sure. It might, for all he knew, be a bare patch in the ground. Objects were deceptive; they never seemed to be what they were. But the wood looked warm and safe. Porter wished he were there, that the whole platoon were there. The wood meant safety from the planes, and the planes would be coming soon. The planes always came soon.

"I never saw anything like it." Hoskins said. "I never saw anything like it in my life. Everybody's gone away. They forgot us. They don't want us in the war. Halverson must be playing blackjack down in the barges."

He yawned.

"Archimbeau," Porter said. "Go take a look down there, Archimbeau."

Archimbeau rose leisurely and started back toward the beach.

"Go on your gut," Porter said. "And leave your gun here. Nobody's going to shoot you."

"Why the gut, then?" Archimbeau wanted to know.

"Because I said the gut," Porter said.

Archimbeau got down on his stomach as soon as he was out of the little hollow and out in the open. He had about fifty yards to go, and every ten feet or so he stopped and listened. The platoon watched him as he worked his tortuous way toward the top of the little ridge. Finally he disappeared in a slight dip.

"When do we eat, Porter?" Trasker asked. "I'm hungry as hell."

"You've got your rations," Porter said. "You can eat when you want to. They're your rations. Nobody's going to take them away from you."

"Every god-damned squad ought to have a god-damned cook go along with them," Private Lang said. "That's the only way to run a god-damned Army."

"Do you think he'll find him?" Porter said to Tyne.

Tyne was pulling blades of grass from the ground and putting them in a little pile. "Find who?"

"Archimbeau. Halverson, for God's sake," Porter said. "Who did you think I was talking about?"

"Oh," Tyne said. He pulled out some more blades of grass. "I don't know."

"Nobody ever finds anybody," said Hoskins.

"What do you think, Tyne?" Porter asked. "For Christ's sake, what do you think?"

"About what?"

"The situation."

Tyne stopped pulling out blades of grass. "Just what is the situation, Eddie?"

"All I know is what Halverson told me. We've got to go up a road for six miles until we run into a farmhouse. Then we stop. That's all I know about it. That's all Halverson knows about it. For all I know, that's all the lieutenant knew about it. Six miles is a long way to go, especially to get to a farmhouse. We aren't a whole battalion, for Christ's sake. And it's a long way from the water."

"What's the house for?" Hoskins asked.

"It beats me," Sergeant Porter said. "Maybe it commands a road or something. If they want a bridgehead they're spreading it pretty thin. If Halverson can't find the captain we're in a hell of a hole."

"Take it easy, Eddie," Tyne said. "Nothing's gone wrong yet. We haven't been here very long. How about a cigarette?"

Porter looked at the brightening landscape around him. "Anyone who wants to smoke can smoke," he said.

Rivera punched Friedman in the ribs. "A butt," he said.

"What happened to the one I gave you last night?"

"I sent it home. They're cutting down on the butts at home. A butt."

Friedman gave him one.

"A match," Rivera said. "Thanks. It pays to have friends."

A figure was crawling along toward them from the direction of the beach, moving forward on his elbows, with a sidewise motion of the knees. Archimbeau.

He came back much faster than he had gone, his face serious, the front of his uniform dark and damp with dew. As he reached the hollow he rose to his feet, brushing at his chest.

"What's the dope?" Sergeant Porter said.

"Damned if I know," Archimbeau said. "I didn't

see Halverson anywheres. They're bringing down some wounded now—"

"From where?" Porter asked.

"They ran into some trouble with that machine-gun. Some Jerries just happened to be driving by with that machine-gun, so they opened up. I was talking to a couple of guys down there."

"How about Halverson?"

"I told you I don't know anything about Halverson or the captain or nobody. I saw Mac, though. He says the lieutenant's dying. Mac says if the lieutenant dies he'll go look for Halverson. The god-damned ocean's full of stuff now. I guess they're bringing in the rolling-stock. The heavy stuff, they're bringing in. The damned place is crawling."

Tyne took a drag from his cigarette and blew it out slowly. "How does the beach look?" he asked.

"Empty. They're bringing in some wounded, though."

"Where was the machine-gun?" Porter asked.

"They didn't tell me. Over there somewhere." Archimbeau gestured vaguely.

"Maybe there's a road over there," said Sergeant Porter.

It was strange to be so close to things and yet to be so far away. That was war. That was always war. It was confused and it was incoherent and it was unreasonable. Nothing ever happened quite on time, nothing ever happened exactly as was expected. War, itself a paradox, was full of paradoxes. A platoon of men, in on the first landing on an enemy coast, could be completely bypassed by events. They could sit in a hollow while all around them things went, or should be going, according to plan, and while the platoon, itself an integral part of the whole operation, seemed to be entirely forgotten. Yet, had the platoon been unnecessary, it might very well have found itself caught underneath shells and planes, with machine-guns and mortars and tanks battering away at it from all directions. The men of the Quartermaster Corps, who appear to lead quiet lives, unscarred by battle, could tell stories of just such occasions. They happen all the time. They probably always have happened.

War, without virtue in itself, breeds virtue. It breeds patience in the impatient and heroism in the cowardly. But mostly it breeds patience. For war is a dull business, the dullest business on earth. War is a period of waiting. Each day of it is crammed with the little hesitations of men uncertain of themselves and awed by the ghastly responsibilities—responsibilities of life and death, the responsibilities of gods—that have been thrust into their hands. The soldier waits for food, for clothing, for a letter, for a battle to begin. And often the food never is served, the clothing is never issued, the letter never arrives, and the battle never begins. The soldier learns to wait meekly, hoping that something will happen. And when the period of waiting is at an end the something that does happen isn't what he expected. So in the end he learns to wait and expect nothing. That is patience, God's one great gift to the soldier.

But he refuses to confess his patience. He curses the fact that he has to wait. He howls at those who cause the waiting. He swears at himself for being such a fool as to wait. And that too is good, in a way. For the man who waits silently is not a good soldier. He is no more than a stone.

"They think I'm going to spend my life here, they're crazy," Private Judson said.

"Take the subway home," said Private Friedman. "Here's a nickel. It's the only nickel I got. It's my last tie with the States. Take it. It's yours. It's worth it to get rid of you."

"Take a tank for a franc," Rivera said.

"A poet," Friedman said. "A Shakespeare. The bard of Avenue A. The card of Avenue A."

"You guys kill me," said Archimbeau.

"He's worked to death," Friedman said. "He's got those open period blues. He had to crawl down to Jones Beach for a little reconnoiter and he's worked to death. He wouldn't have kicked if it had been Coney Island."

"Do it yourself," Archimbeau said. "When I'm out of the Army and you're sweating it off in Tibet you'll be laughing out of the other side of your face."

"For Christ's sake, Sergeant," Trasker said to Porter, "how long are we going to stay here? My tail's cold."

"We'll stay till it freezes to the ground," Porter said. "There's a lot there to spare."

"Got any ideas where to go, Trasker?" Sergeant Hoskins asked.

"Pike's Peak," Trasker said. "If I was there I'd run up backwards."

"I'd go up on my hands, pushing a peanut with my nose," Archimbeau said. "And then I'd take a train."

"The railroads are jammed these days," Rivera said.

"Oh, for Christ's sake," Porter said. He got to his feet. "Come on over here with me, Hoskins," he said. "You, too, Bill." He walked a few yards away and leaned against the bole of a tree.

Hoskins and Tyne followed him. Tyne left the map case behind him.

"Look," Porter said in a low voice, "something's wrong. I know something's wrong. Halverson shouldn't have taken so long to find the captain. I don't know what he did. Maybe he went looking for him over there. And if he did, God knows when he'll get back. Am I right?"

"It sounds right," Tyne said very precisely. Hoskins nodded solemnly.

"There's no sense in it," Porter went on. "There's no sense in it at all. Now, we know where to go, or at least we think we know where to go, and if we hang around here any longer we'll screw up the whole works."

"Planes will be over pretty soon," Hoskins said. His voice was almost sad.

"Sure as hell they will," Porter agreed. "And sure as hell they're going to send a few tanks along here pretty soon, while we're still up in the god-damned air. My idea is that we ought to leave someone here in case Halverson shows up, and go ahead ourselves while he's waiting. Six miles is a hell of a long way."

"A hell of a long way," Hoskins said.

"What do you think?"

"It's up to you, Eddie," Tyne said carefully. "You know what you're doing."

Hoskins nodded his head without saying anything.

"I've got to know," Porter said.

"Do it, then," Tyne said. "I've got something . . ." he started to say.

Porter held up his hand, palm outward, and Tyne broke off in the middle of his sentence. "Listen," Porter said.

The platoon, which had been talking among itself while watching the non-commissioned officers, was suddenly silent. Hoskins stood with his head cocked slightly to one side. He ran his tongue over his lips.

"Hear anything?" Porter asked.

From somewhere came a faint thunder. It was hard to ascertain the exact direction of the sound.

"God-damned guns," Hoskins said.

"Hey, Sergeant, it's guns," Rivera called.

"Where they coming from?" Porter asked. "They're coming from out to sea, aren't they?"

"I think so," Tyne said. The sea was the only logical place, unless another landing had been made somewhere along the coast and had run into trouble.

"Ack-ack," Hoskins said.

"You sure?" Porter wanted to know.

"Tolerable sure," said Hoskins.

Sergeant Porter moved away from the tree and threw his shoulders back as though his neck were sore. "That's it, then."

"Must be ships shooting at planes," Hoskins said.

"That's the way it is," said Porter. "That's sure as hell the way it is. Come on."

He went back to the platoon. "All right, off and on," he said. "We're going over in the woods. Squad columns. Hop to it, for Christ's sake."

Archimbeau was doubtful. "How do we know those ain't our planes?"

"Because the ships are ours, dope," Trasker told him. "We got the only ships on the water. I wouldn't be a sailor for nothing."

The platoon got to its feet in a hurry. Hoskins whistled up his squad, and Sergeant Ward, who was quiet and kept out of things, who had sat quietly on the fringe of the gathering, picked up his carbine and spoke a quiet order.

"Who's going to stay here, Eddie?" Tyne asked.

"Stay here for what?" Porter asked. He wanted to get to the woods in a hurry.

"Halverson."

Porter's hand flickered impatiently. "I don't know," he said.

"I'll stay," Tyne said. "I've got nothing to do."

Porter smiled at him quickly. "Okay," he said. "Okay. You stay here. For Christ's sake, get moving, God damn it. We haven't got all day. Get those squads moving. Spread 'em out. You stay here, Bill. We'll be over in the woods."

"Leave me your glasses, will you?"

"Sure." Porter lifted the strap over his head and passed Tyne his binoculars. "Help yourself. We'll be over in the woods. Let's go."

The platoon moved out of the hollow, fanning out as it went. It was clear going all the way to the woods. Tyne watched the backs of the men as they receded from him. Once Porter yelled something up the line, but he could not make out what it was. The words ran together as the wind increased in the trees. The platoon reached the line of woods, and one by one the men vanished into the foliage.

It seemed very silent in the hollow. Where there had been whispering and the sound of voices there was nothing but a rustling of leaves. Far away, somewhere beyond the world of that moment, the guns continued to bark out at something in the sky. Tyne sighed, lit a cigarette, and lay down on his stomach. Then, as though he were doing a guilty act, he snuffed the cigarette out on the ground. He propped himself on his elbows, took off his helmet, and began focusing the binoculars on the sky beyond the ridge that hid the beach from his sight. He thought he could hear the motors of planes, but he wasn't sure.

Then he remembered that the map case, which he was planning to give Porter, was still with him—was, as a matter of fact, lying underneath his legs, with the strap caught on a tiny shrub. He looked at his watch. It was 0817. Precisely.

# 3

McWILLIAMS CAME walking over the ridge as though he were looking for daisies. He had a long, thin head that made his helmet appear much bigger and broader than it was. Had his helmet jogged up and down over his eyes as he walked it would have seemed perfectly in order. His fatigues were too small for him, and his skinny wrists jutted out from the curtailed sleeves like the obscene legs of a dressed chicken.

McWilliams paid no attention to the war. He took it as it came. He asked questions, but not because he was interested. It was merely because he wanted to be absolutely sure of everything that concerned him. The war as a whole was nothing to McWilliams; it was the little things that mattered. If McWilliams came walking over a ridge in a battle area instead of crawling on his belly, it meant that he had turned the whole situation over in his mind and had decided that there was no danger involved if Ransom McWilliams walked upright over a ridge in a battle area. If he had decided that it was all right to walk into the arms of

Satan himself, he would have done just that. He was slow and he was Southern and he was dependable. Once McWilliams was told to do a thing he did it. He was a good man to have around.

As he came into the hollow Tyne rose up to meet him. McWilliams looked around him curiously. "Where's everybody?" he asked.

"Gone into the woods," Tyne said. "Planes are headed this way."

"Yeah," McWilliams said. "I heard the guns."

He sat down beside Tyne.

"The lieutenant's dead," he said.

"Too bad," Tyne said.

McWilliams stared at Tyne solemnly. "I suppose so," he said. "Halverson's dead, too. Deader than hell and Jesus."

Tyne, for no particular reason, felt as though he had received a punch in the solar plexus. After a moment he said "Is he?"

"Uh-huh," McWilliams said. "Machine-gun got him. He was looking for the captain, and they stitched him right across the middle."

"How do you know?" Tyne asked.

"Tolliver told me. You know Tolliver? B Company. He saw Halverson."

"What about the captain?"

"I don't know anything about the captain."

Tyne stared at the binoculars in his hand. That left it up to Porter, all the way around. The situation, which had seemed to be more or less in hand, was no longer good. The situation was deteriorating rapidly. "God damn it to hell," he said to himself, but aloud.

"What?"

"Nothing. What's going on down there?"

A package of cigarettes was in McWilliams's hand. "Mind if I smoke?" he said. "Is it okay? Okay. They're bringing in the big stuff. Transports and Christ knows what else down there. Everywhere you look. I heard those guns. Planes 're coming in, all right. Be here pretty soon."

"Pretty soon," Tyne said. He peered through the binoculars again. As he did so he thought of Lieutenant Rand, trying to see the guns flash through the night. It had been a very silly thing to do. Probably no more silly, though, than trying to see a plane when you couldn't even hear a plane.

"I'm glad I'm not down on the beach any more," McWilliams said. "That place is sure going to get hell strafed out of it. It sure is."

"We'd better be getting over in the woods," Tyne said. "The planes will be here in a minute."

There was a high whine that came into the air unexpectedly. It sounded quite near, as though a lot of planes were flying very high almost overhead.

"There they are," McWilliams said. "Put out that butt."

"Can't see a light in daylight."

"They can see smoke."

Anti-aircraft guns went off very near at hand, beyond the ridge that cut off the sea. The transports and their escort were going into action. The guns beat out a fast tattoo, in pairs, whumping their shells up into the air as fast as they could throw them into the breech and slam it shut. "Noisy," McWilliams said. "You know that god-damned lieutenant never moved his hands? Never moved them."

There were five deep explosions that reverberated over the ridge. One of the enemy planes, wherever it was, had dropped a stick among the transports. All the explosions, however, had sounded exactly like each other. The plane must have missed. The guns snapped on.

Another stick came down, and this time a deeper roar went with it. Over the ridge a black mushroom of smoke raced toward the reaches of the air. That was no miss, no miss at all. The air rolled back across the little hollow. A hot wind struck the trees.

"Hit something that time," McWilliams said.

"We'd better sit tight here," Tyne said. "There may be a few fighters around somewhere. I don't want any fighters to catch me in an open field."

"I don't want any fighters to catch me in an open field, neither," McWilliams said. "I wonder what the hell's happening down there now."

"Plenty," said Tyne. "Plenty of plenty."

This was it, the way it was expected to be. This was what might have happened during the landing itself. Tyne found himself thinking of the coast of France. He had never seen that coast, but he imagined that now it was just one long concrete wall, bristling with guns. They would set the water afire with oil, too. They would do everything they could. When that day came, Tyne wanted to be somewhere else, far, far away. This, in itself, was bad enough. And even this was mild. In this you knew where everything was. You were here and the bombs were there. It all fitted beautifully together. You were here and the bombs were there. Nothing could have been simpler. In the transports men were being killed, but they weren't you. You were where you were and the men who were being killed were where they were. It had even been worse in London. Then you knew where you were, but you never knew where the bombs were. Now you had a grandstand view. The only trouble was that you couldn't see anything. Very little is seen in war, anyway. Wars are fought by ear.

"I'd like to see that," McWilliams said. The black column of smoke soared higher. Over the roar of the guns there was a series of minor explosions that weren't bombs but very likely were exploding ammunition. There couldn't be many planes in the sky, though, because only two sticks had been dropped; not many planes, that is, unless they were taking their time and making several runs and putting them where they hurt. "Wonder where our planes are," McWilliams said.

"They'll be along."

"They're taking their time."

"They have a lot of it."

But there should have been air support. By rights there shouldn't be an enemy plane in the sky. Tyne couldn't understand it. The only solution seemed to be that this landing was a feint, a diversion. Perhaps the main landing had been made somewhere else, and all the planes had gone there. The planes did, after all, have a long distance to come. With the gas a fighter got it couldn't do much more than arrive, turn around, and go back. It must be that this landing had

44

been a diversion. Yet the water was supposed to be jammed with ships. McWilliams had said so, and Mc-Williams had seen them. It didn't make sense. It couldn't be that the planes had missed the bus.

Another stick of bombs fell. The planes sounded lower.

"Can I go take a look, Corporal?"

"You stay the hell where you are. I want you here." The binoculars were absolutely useless. Tyne could see absolutely nothing in the sky. Puffs of ack-ack, that was all. But no planes. He was glad that the trees gave him some cover. You never could tell, though. Let the bombardier up there, whatever he was, be a fraction of an inch off, and they might not even find your dog-tags. Unconsciously Tyne pressed his body into the earth as though he hoped the ground would gape open and swallow him.

Earth is a marvelous thing. A man does not appreciate earth, just ordinary dirt, until he has been under fire. Then, when he feels that three inches of dry sod scraped up in front of his eyes gives him adequate protection, dirt comes into its own. Foxholes can be dug in it; slit trenches can be dug in it. An hour's work can make enough protection to outlast the worst possible bombing attack. If the hole is deep enough a tank will pass over it, and all the man in the hole will have to do is duck his head a little. And even when there is no cover, absolutely none, a man can feel life surging through him if he just hugs the ground. And he will feel that if he stretched out his arms he could draw in the whole world and hold it to his chest.

Through the eyepieces of the binoculars Tyne at

45

last saw the planes, six of them, in two V's flying very high, looking completely unwarlike, completely out of things. It did not seem possible that such minute instruments could do so much damage. They reminded him of stuffed swans that glide over a stage setting, or perhaps in a ballet. They were out of the picture. They held no meaning. They were too far away to hold any meaning at all; one could not connect them with the bombs. Tyne had found them by following the ack-ack puffs.

"I see the planes," he said. "Six of them."

"That all?" McWilliams asked. "Not many, is it? You'd think they'd have a couple of hundred around up there: It just goes to show you."

"It just goes to show you what?"

McWilliams looked at him owlishly. "It just goes to show you," he repeated.

"It's funny," Tyne said. "Maybe there 're more coming." He swerved the binoculars behind the ack-ack bursts, hoping to pick up more planes. There were none.

"I tell you what, Corporal," McWilliams said slowly. "I got an idea. What say I take the glasses and go over on the ridge there and take a look at the water? We ought to know what's going on, hadn't we? I think we ought to know what's going on."

"We know what's going on," Tyne said. "There's no point in it."

"You never can tell," McWilliams said.

"We've got to be getting along to the platoon," said Tyne.

"You wouldn't go through an open field with those

planes up there, would you, Corporal? I wouldn't do that."

"No, I wouldn't either," Tyne admitted.

The anti-aircraft fire stopped without warning. Evidently the bombers were out of range. It was odd that they had passed on after only dropping two sticks; it increased Tyne's feeling that this landing had been a feint. The bombers had probably gone on after bigger game. There must be a more important landing taking place farther down the coast. A few odd pieces of shrapnel smashed down around them.

"They ought to know," McWilliams said.

"Who ought to know?"

"The guys," said McWilliams. "Suppose I went and took a look over the ridge. Maybe there's a new landing coming off. They'd want to know if there was, wouldn't they? It stands to reason."

"Go and take a look, McWilliams," Tyne said. "Go and take a look. Get it off your mind."

McWilliams grinned at him. "It's just for the record," he said. "I think it's a good idea."

"Don't hang around, though. Those bombers may be back." Tyne handed him the binoculars. "Take a good look."

Belly to the ground, McWilliams began worming his way toward the ridge. He was exercising caution, now that there were planes around. McWilliams might have ideas, but he was nobody's fool. Once he got an idea in his head it was hard to get it out. And McWilliams had an idea he wanted to see what was going on in the water; the easiest way was to let him see. Tyne watched him crawling, and he could im-

47

agine his face. McWilliams's jaw would be jutted out slightly and his mouth would be open about an inch. Tyne remembered McWilliams's face on a day when it had looked just like that. It had been in Sicily, and McWilliams, as a runner, had come crawling up to a slit trench where Tyne was sitting. His jaw had jutted out and his mouth had been open. It was his special expression that he saved for crawling. He made it look hard.

He was halfway across the open space to the ridge when the anti-aircraft guns opened up again, and when they did he hesitated for a moment and looked back. Tyne neither shouted nor made a gesture. He lay flat, trying to see the sky and McWilliams all at the same time. McWilliams continued his crawl.

By the time he reached the ridge the third stick of bombs had fallen. Tyne could not tell whether they had hit anything or not. McWilliams sprawled on the ridge, legs apart, focusing on the ships. Once he turned around and shook his head violently. The movement was meaningless to Tyne. It couldn't mean that nothing had been hit, because the smoke from some ship or other was still moving up the sky. Perhaps it was a signal that nothing was coming ashore at the time. A shake of the head could mean a thousand things. But Tyne could not think of one.

Silence came almost like a clap of thunder; the guns stopped as though a great hand had been placed over their mouths. A new note came into the air, high-pitched, fierce. Fighters.

"Come on back," Tyne yelled.

McWilliams turned, waved his hand, and pointed

up in the air. He shook his head again. Far up in the sky the rattle of a machine-gun could be heard. Immediately afterwards a comet of smoke appeared high over the water. It described a painfully slow parabola toward the ground and then disappeared behind the wide cloud of smoke that was rising from the wounded ship. The air cover had at last arrived. The ships were holding fire for fear they would hit one of their own planes. McWilliams followed the falling plane with the binoculars as it appeared on the other side of the smoke and plummeted into the sea. When it had passed out of sight he turned around and waved his hand in a small, violent circle. It was his accolade. More machine-guns were sounding up in the sky.

Tyne began to feel very uncomfortable. He wished that McWilliams would come back, that he were in the woods with the platoon, that something would happen that would be right. The feeling was growing on him that nothing had been right so far. Everything was wrong. His position was wrong. McWilliams, with the binoculars to his eyes, was wrong. The whole landing had been wrong. He felt, rather foolishly, as though he had come to a summer resort for a vacation, a summer resort than he didn't like. The people were not the kind of people he had expected to find, and there was a director of athletics who made him indulge in games that held no interest for him. Even the swimming was bad. He noted that his hunger, which had cut him a little while ago, had completely vanished. Now, on the contrary, he felt slightly nauseated, as though he had eaten too much. It was hard for the body to keep up with things. The body was a backward instrument.

"Come back, McWilliams," he called.

McWilliams's voice came across to him clearly. "In a minute, Corporal."

The planes moved across the sky. It was impossible to tell their position by the sound of their motors, but they seemed to be going toward the north. Occasionally a machine-gun would chatter, like a riveting machine far away. The sun was full up in the sky, glancing off the wet leaves, drying the dew. Tyne could feel that his knees, where he had been lying, were wet.

"Come on back, McWilliams," Tyne called again.

He could almost hear McWilliams sigh as he took the binoculars from his eyes, turned his body around, and began the tedious crawl back to the hollow.

Tyne saw the planes coming a long way off—three fighters, Messerschmitt 110's. They were coming along the coastline from the north, flying very fast, and very low. They couldn't have been more than a hundred feet off the ground. He watched them coming in the same way a bird must watch a snake. They seemed to be coming right at him, and he couldn't move. Their silhouettes swelled on the horizon, over the level earth. At what must have been the far end of the beach, perhaps a mile away, they started firing. They were strafing the barges.

There was no anti-aircraft fire. The planes were too low, they had come too suddenly, hedgehopping, and any shrapnel from the anti-aircraft might have caught the men on the beach. The Messerschmitts roared along, all guns chattering, unopposed. McWilliams saw them coming almost at the same time as Tyne did. He turned to look at them almost casually, as though they were annoying flies. Then, when they started to fire their guns, he leaped up and ran for the hollow. He had gone perhaps twenty feet when the planes were upon him. Tyne could see the earth fly as their bullets cut a swath through it. McWilliams suddenly faced the planes and flung his arms in front of him as though the gesture could ward them off. Then he went back a few paces and collapsed with his arms still out-flung. He too had been stitched. Right up the middle.

After he had fallen Tyne cried out "McWilliams!" His voice was lost in the roar of the receding planes. "Son of a bitch!" he screamed after them. "Son of a bitch." He grabbed his rifle and fired three rapid shots after them. Foolish. The Messerschmitts went down the coast about three miles, went into an Immelmann, and came back along the beach. Tyne fired the rest of his magazine at them when they were still out of range and then threw himself down behind a tree. The ma-chine-guns opened up again. He watched the planes, fascinated. One track of bullets cut the ground per-haps three feet from McWilliams's body.

As the Messerschmitts passed to the north end of the beach one of them soared up, banked leisurely, and came back, this time behind Tyne. He scrambled around to watch it. The plane cut in very low over the woods where the platoon was hiding and opened up. Even from a distance of two hundred yards Tyne could see the tops of the trees quiver and shake as the bullets smashed into and through them. He felt completely lost. The Messerschmitt came back over the woods and started to rake it again, but this time the machine-guns stopped almost as soon as they had begun. The plane had evidently run out of ammunition. It disappeared over some foothills to the northeast.

For a moment after the planes had gone Tyne sat stupefied. The attack had shocked him. Planes always did. They were an impossible, unimaginable force. He could understand men against men, and even men against tanks, but planes were something else again. He had once read a fantastic story about gigantic insects that turned against man; the planes were those insects. Tanks, which could be taken for gigantic beetles, were terrifying too in their way, but one always knew that inside the tanks were men, and men were vulnerable. But the planes moved too fast. It was impossible to conceive of any human being, any human element, hidden in their bowels and controlling them. They had a life of their own, vindictive, murderous. Even his own planes made Tyne feel uncomfortable.

For nearly three minutes he remained where he was, sitting up with his back against a tree. Over the ridge he could hear sounds from the beach. Men were shouting. Someone was screaming in a high-pitched voice. It sounded almost like a woman.

Deliberately Tyne rose to his feet and walked out into the open where McWilliams was lying. As soon as he saw the body he knew that there was nothing to be done. There is something about a dead man's face that cannot be explained. Something has gone from the features. It is as though life lent an aura, a glow, that, unseen, could yet be perceived through some unknown sense. The face of a dead man resembles what the dead man is—a lump of clay. The face somehow merges with the earth. Clothes hang awkwardly on the body and bunch up strangely; the clothes seem foreign to the body that is wearing them.

That was the way it was with McWilliams. Looking at his face, Tyne could not conceive that he had ever known him, that he had ever eaten and talked with him. He knew that there was no need to touch the body to see if life still existed. McWilliams's eyes were wide open. Blood seeped through the front of his fatigues. One of the bullets had gone through his neck; there was a lot of blood there. Tyne had seen much of death, but he had never reconciled himself to it. Death was indecent, obscene. There was something naked about a body, the nakedness of being unsouled, and there is no deeper nakedness than that.

There was no time for Tyne to muse on the incontrovertible fact of death, even had he wanted to. He stared down at McWilliams's body for a moment and then looked hesitatingly at the ridge. It might be a good idea to take a quick look at the beach. The wounded man was still screaming. He heard a deep voice call "Bring it up, bring it up!" Instead of mounting the ridge, however, he walked over to where McWilliams had dropped his rifle. Tyne laid his own rifle down carefully and picked up McWilliams's. There was no explanation for his action; he just did it. Then he turned on his heel, walked back to the hollow, picked up the map case, and went out in the open field toward the wood.

As he walked he lit a cigarette. He was a very much frightened young man.

# 4

TRASKER WAS dead. Sergeant Hoskins had a bullet in the calf of his left leg, and Private Giorgio, of Sergeant Ward's squad, had a smashed shoulder. The platoon had got off easily. The pilot of the Messerschmitt had seen something gleam in the woods. No one knew what it was, but the pilot must have seen something; otherwise he wouldn't have taken the crack at them. If he hadn't run out of ammunition it might have been worse. As it was, the platoon never knew what hit them. They had not seen the plane come over. They had heard it machine-gunning the beaches, but when it went after the woods the trees had hid it from their sight until the bullets started to smash down among them. They had been very lucky.

Trasker had taken a slug in the mouth. He had been talking to Archimbeau—talking in a loud voice, because the planes were making a lot of noise—when they got him. He had started to say "For Christ's sake, Arch—" but he had never got any farther. It was an odd thing to say as one's last words, but that was just the way it was. Archimbeau felt very badly about it. When Trasker had fallen over he had reached out to grab him, and then he saw where the wound was, so he didn't bother. There was no point in it, once you saw the wound. They hadn't even been able to shoot at the plane; they hadn't seen it.

Hoskins knew it was a Messerschmitt that had put the hole in him, because Hoskins was an old soldier and he knew things like that. It was his business to know them. Some of the men in the platoon, Giorgio for instance, might never know who or what had shot them, because their minds didn't run in that direction. But Hoskins knew. He wasn't in any real pain—not yet, anyway. The wound wasn't such a bad one, but the muscles were torn and he couldn't walk. He bandaged the wound himself.

"Does it hurt?" Porter asked. Porter was a little shaken by the strafing. He had not expected it, and it preyed upon his mind. He believed that it was his fault, for it was he who had considered the wood a safe place; he had brought the platoon there.

"It don't hurt yet," Hoskins said, "but it god-damned well will."

"It's a Purple Heart, Sarge," Rivera said.

"Shove it," Sergeant Hoskins said. "Next Messerschmitt pilot I see I'm going to shoot all by myself. Bastards."

"What are you going to do?" Porter asked.

"Stay here, for God's sake," said Hoskins. "What the hell did you think I was going to do? Get up a god-damned football game?" The wound had angered him and made him loquacious.

"Giorgio got shot in the shoulder," Porter said.

"Who the hell cares?" said Hoskins.

Archimbeau sat looking at Trasker. Friedman came over and patted his shoulder. "He was a good guy," Archimbeau said.

"Okay," said Friedman.

"No Tibet," Archimbeau said.

"Okay."

"I wish Halverson would show up," Sergeant Porter said.

The platoon was spread out, sitting against trees. They felt beat up. Everything seemed to be going wrong. Nothing good had happened. It had been bad in the hollow and it was bad under the trees. The platoon wanted to move. The men were restless. They didn't care where they went; they just wanted to be on the move. Each knew that events were taking place that were bypassing them; they were in a stagnant pool, and all around them flood waters were rushing toward an unknown and dangerous destination. One or two of them, for want of something better to do, were eating C rations. Everyone was keyed up.

"We can't stay here all day, Eddie," Sergeant Ward said.

"I know it, for God's sake," Porter said. "But what can I do?"

Sergeant Ward thought a minute. "I don't know," he said.

"How's Giorgio?"

"He can walk. It's not too bad."

"Hell of a thing."

Rivera was talking to Private Rankin, who was an automatic rifleman.

"You want to live here?" he said.

"I didn't say I wanted to live here," Rankin said.

"It's a nice country," Rivera said. "Full of opportunity. Just look around you. Opportunity, that's the big thing."

"The hell with the country," Rankin said.

"That's a lousy way to talk about a country where you're a guest. They'll kick you the hell out."

"No they won't," said Private Rankin.

"Do you know who you're fighting?" Rivera asked.

"They never told me. Germans."

Rivera spat on the ground. "That's all I want to know."

Rankin didn't understand him. "You're screwy," he said.

"It's life," said Rivera.

Archimbeau was walking around with his hands in his pockets, kicking dead leaves. His rifle was slung over his shoulder. "We were the same draft board," he said. "The same day."

"Forget it," Friedman said. He left Archimbeau and walked over to Rivera.

"Go away," Rivera said. "A butt."

Friedman gave him a cigarette. "Arch is taking it hard."

"Nobody dies," said Rivera. It was a platoon cliché.

Sergeant Porter had just about made up his mind. There was nothing for it but to move on. It was the best thing to do. There was no sense in waiting for Halverson, because Halverson obviously wasn't coming. He wondered what was keeping Tyne; probably he was holing in, figuring that the planes would be back. Holing in, that is, if the planes hadn't got him, too.

There was a sound of someone coming through the bushes. Porter pointed his carbine in the direction of the sound. "Halt," he said. The movement stopped. "Who's there?"

"Tyne."

"Well, come on, for God's sake. Where have you been?"

Tyne came into view. The platoon looked at him with interest. Some of the men came over to him. "What happened?" Porter asked.

Tyne was still smoking his cigarette. Before answering he took out another and lit it from the stub of the first. He noticed that his hand was trembling; so did the men around him.

"Halverson's dead," he said.

"God damn," Porter said. "What happened?"

"Machine-gun got him."

"Plane?"

"No, the one that was down there."

"Bad," Porter said.

"McWilliams is dead, too. The plane got him. And the lieutenant died."

Porter frowned. It was up to him now. "That does it," he said. "Trasker's dead here. Hoskins and Giorgio got wounded."

"I've got the lieutenant's map case."

"Get it from the barge?"

"No, I had it all the time. I was going to give it to you."

As Tyne handed him the case Porter stared at it as

though he could not believe it existed. It was a shiny new map case; Lieutenant Rand had never really had a chance to use it. The leather gleamed, but in one place there was a long deep scratch down the side.

"What's in it?" Porter asked.

"I don't know," Tyne said. "Look and see."

Porter unbuckled it and looked inside. He pulled out two pieces of paper. One was a detail map of a limited area; the other was a rough penciled sketch of what looked on first glance like a road junction.

Slowly and deliberately Porter fell on his knees and spread out the large map. The whole platoon gathered around him then, those nearest the map falling on their knees, too, and those behind them looking over the first rank's shoulders. The map was of the district where they were. There was the seacoast. There was the beach. There was the wood where they were. "There's the road," Porter said. He put his finger on it. Judging from the map, it was about a hundred yards to the south of the little wood. Halverson's calculations had been slightly off.

"Where's the farmhouse?" Tyne asked.

Porter traced the road with his forefinger. "Here," he said. "This must be it. It's the only house. Let's see, where's the scale? It's about six miles, all right."

"Nearer seven," Ward said. "What's the other thing?"

The penciled sketch was spread out over the big map. "It's the farmhouse," Porter said. "What's that?" He pointed toward a series of concentric broken lines.

"Rocks," Tyne said. "High ground."

"It's marked for a machine-gun," Porter said. "One

of the farm buildings is marked for a machine-gun too."

"That's me," Rivera said. "I like to work indoors.'

"There's no god-damned orders," Porter said. "Just this."

"Have to do," said Ward.

"He must have swallowed the orders," Porter said "Too many secrets in this bloody war."

"Porter," Hoskins called. "Bring it over here and let me see it."

Porter picked up the two maps and carried them over to where Hoskins was sitting with his back against a tree. Hoskins took the map, and as he studied it he grimaced. His teeth showed black between his lips

"Giving you trouble?" Porter asked.

"It will," Hoskins said. "That bridge."

"What about it?"

"You'll have to blow it."

Porter frowned over the map. "Yes. Blow it," he said.

"You have to use grenades. They'll bring up stuff over that bridge."

"Your leg hurting now?"

"Son of a bitch. God-damned Heinie bastards. Grenades will do it, all right. Take time, though."

Hoskins tossed the maps aside as though he were annoyed with them. "Leave me some water," he said. "I may be here quite a while."

"Want someone to take you down to the beach?" Porter was solicitous. He hated to lose Hoskins.

"Like hell. They'll be strafing that place for weeks. I'm going to stay right here."

"What about Giorgio?"

"The hell with Giorgio. Jesus, Porter, you're in command. Don't ask so many christly questions. Leave me alone."

Porter picked up the maps and walked back to where the platoon was gathered. He folded the maps and put them carefully back in his case. "Cousins, go ask Giorgio if he can get back to the beach by himself," he said.

As Cousins rose artillery fire came to their ears from the north. It was light stuff, coming from inland. As they listened they heard shells exploding near by. A machine-gun began far away; another joined it. The battle was beginning.

"We've got to get moving," Porter said. Another shell exploded quite near them. A few of the men ducked involuntarily.

Cousins came back. He had been eating his rations before Tyne had returned, and now he was sucking on a lemon drop from the ration. "Giorgio says the hell with the beach," he said. "He wants to go along."

"He can't go along," Porter said. "They'll be setting up a hospital here pretty soon. Tell him to stay here."

"Tell him yourself," Cousins said. "You've got the rank."

Porter stared fiercely at Cousins, opened his mouth to say something, and then walked over to Giorgio. "You'd better go down to the beach, Giorgio," he said.

"Listen," Giorgio said, "I'm wounded. I got privileges. I don't want to go down to the beach. I want to go along."

"You can't go along. You won't do any good. You can't do anything."

"Oh, for Christ's sake."

"Go on down to the beach."

"I'll stay here with the sergeant."

"Suit yourself," Porter said. "Tyne, where are the binoculars?"

"Oh, God," Tyne said, "I forgot them. McWilliams has them."

"The only pair we had," Porter said. "They aren't doing him any good."

"I'll go back," Tyne said.

"Never mind," Porter said. He walked over and picked up his carbine, which he had laid down while he was going over the maps. "Let's go," he said. "We're going to move."

"For Christ's sake, roll Trasker over," Hoskins said. "I don't want to have to look at that mug for two days."

Archimbeau rolled Trasker's body over. His face was set as he did it.

"Sunny Italy," Rivera said. He picked up his barrel. "A little hike."

"You should have to carry this," Friedman said. He was an ammunition carrier. He did not like the job.

"I am happy with you, dear," Rivera said. "You make me very happy."

"After the war I will cut you dead on the street," Friedman said.

"After the war I will never go to Jersey City to give you a chance to cut me dead," said Rivera.

"Listen," Porter said. "When we hit the road we'll go in three squads. We'll bust Hoskins's squad up.

Corporal Kramer, divide them in three. My squad will go first. Archimbeau and Cousins will be scouts. Rankin, follow them. Ward, you take the second squad after me. Tyne, you take the third. Kramer, you're Tyne's assistant squad leader. You bring up the rear. Get it?"

There were murmurs of assent.

"Now, for Christ's sake, keep your eyes open. God only knows what might be coming down the road. If they bring—" A shell struck near the wood. "If they bring up tanks they'll probably bring them along the road. Be ready to fan out at any time. If you hear me blow my whistle, head for cover. And I mean cover. Keep your eyes open for planes. They may try to shell the road, too. I don't think they're wide awake yet, but they're going to be. It's a stinking situation. Right?"

"Right!" chorused the platoon.

"Then let's go."

Archimbeau and Cousins started out, and Rankin followed them. While the file of men was moving out Tyne stood uneasily, watching them. A little, seedy man named Johnson slipped over to Hoskins and handed him a letter. "Mail this for me, will you, Sergeant?" he said. Hoskins took it silently, and Johnson slipped into his place in Ward's squad.

Tyne went over to where Hoskins was lying. "How is it, Hosk?" he asked.

Hoskins smiled faintly. "It'll keep," he said. "I've got it on ice."

"Take it easy."

"Tyne, you're a smart apple," Hoskins said. "Keep your head."

"I'm the boy," Tyne said.

"I mean it. Keep your head. You may need it."

"I always have."

A grimace twisted Hoskins's face. "Bloody leg," he said. "I ran into an Australian in Tunis," he said, "and they slugged one into his leg at Mareth. He was always going to walk with a limp. That's a hell of a way to be. Ruins you with the Army."

"You'll be all right, Hosk."

"You're a smart apple. Keep your head on."

Tyne took his canteen from his belt. "Better hang on to this," he said.

"I forgot. Thanks," said Hoskins. "Keep your eye on Porter. I think he's going to crack."

"How do you know?"

"I've seen them crack, for Christ's sake. He's a good man, but I think he's going to crack. That's the way it goes. He's got a lot on his mind. Keep your head on."

"Okay, Hosk."

The last of the three squads was moving out. Tyne took up his place at the rear. He was the last man in the platoon. "See you around, Hosk," he said.

"Yeah," Sergeant Hoskins said. "Around."

The platoon wound through the wood, circling trees, stepping over bushes. Tyne caught one legging in a low thorn and very nearly tripped. He slashed at the thorn with his bayonet. Once he looked back, but he could no longer see Hoskins and Giorgio. They were out of sight behind the trees. When he thought of Giorgio he had to smile. He was an Italian, and his father was fairly fresh from the old country, yet all Giorgio would see of Italy was a beach and a little wood. It was ironic. Tyne, of all the people in the world, had never expected to be in Italy. He had never had the slightest urge to travel; on the contrary, he was a one-town man. Rhode Island might be tiny and Providence might not be much as cities go, but it was all that Tyne wanted. If a war had not come along and pulled the pins from under the quiet life he had led and had wanted to lead, he might have been contented with an existence that contained, as its travel itinerary, three trips to New York City and one two-weeks' sojourn in the Great Smokies. Yet here he was, moving in toward the heart of an enemy country, a country that was a far cry from Rhode Island and Providence, and all the rest of life. Tyne was caught up in a maelstrom, and, though he did not know it, he wanted nothing more in the world than to be able to cry out for help.

They came out of the wood to a rough and dusty field. The sun had already dried the dew, and their feet kicked up small clouds of baked earth. The road cut through the dry field, running toward the north-east. It was little more than a cart track—two deep ruts running through the dull grass. They turned into it in two files, one walking on each side of the road. It was bad going. Carts had passed over the road in wet weather; their wheels had sunk into mud, and the mud had dried, leaving deep welts. To their left the artillery pounded on. Shells were falling behind them and to the north, along the beach and among the ships. The machine-guns sang like locusts in a summer sun.

They were all frightened. The barrage could not

be trusted; it was landing on the beach at the moment, but it might start moving inland at any time. They kept glancing anxiously behind them, as though they were afraid the barrage would move if they didn't watch it. The sun was beginning to bother Porter. He hated heat, and now, with the equipment he was carrying, sweat ran down his face and left pale rivers in the grime along his cheeks. He was still surprised that the sun could achieve so much heat so early in the morning. The six miles ahead of him became an infinity of miles. Before he had gone three hundred yards along the road he was tired. He shifted his carbine from shoulder to shoulder. From time to time he would glance behind him, not so much to watch the barrage as to check on the platoon. The road led up to a slight rise, and from this he could see the beach and the ships lying offshore. Barges were teeming around the transports. Obviously more men were coming ashore. That was the reason for the barrage. In that case, it would probably stay where it was. It wouldn't chase them.

"It could have been something else," Rivera said to Friedman. "It could have been the Engineers or the tanks. It could even have been the Navy. They looked at me and said 'Here's a guy that can walk.' They finished me, all right."

"Everybody walks," Friedman said. "Even monkeys."

"There are limits," Rivera said. "Plenty of limits."

"I've been thinking," said Friedman. "How long have we been in the Army?"

"Jesus," Rivera said. He spat into the dust.

"Look at Hoskins. He gets a lousy little dig in the leg. He's out of the Army. But he doesn't want to be out of the Army."

"Justice," Rivera said.

"Where are we going, Rivera?"

"I am going some place where I can set up this weapon," Rivera said. "And then I am going to shoot this weapon. I am not going to walk any more."

"There are limits," Friedman said.

Why didn't they use paratroops? Porter kept asking himself. The farmhouse, whatever its uses, was far enough inland to use the paratroops. It would have been the most natural thing in the world—just fly over, scatter a few, and let them hold it. God knows it would have saved time, lots of time. As things stood it was nearly ten. Valuable hours had been wasted, had been allowed to run down the drain. Time, that was so precious, had been spent recklessly. It was bad, bad all the way through. They wouldn't reach the farmhouse before noon.

No worries crossed Tyne's mind. For the first time that morning he felt fairly relaxed. As long as he was moving he was quite content. As he walked he looked about him at the country. The land was fairly level, but he figured that in about a half an hour they would run into rather rough-looking foothills. There was little vegetation. It was almost as though the wood where they had stopped had been a freak. A ditch, obscure and ill defined, ran parallel with the road, about fifty feet away. It looked like a trench. In a pinch it could serve for one.

To a man marching in the sun time becomes as static as the shimmering horizon. It surrounds him and presses on his shoulders. He moves, but time stops. Seconds swell to giant size and minutes are immensities. The body conditions the mind's knowledge of time—it flies in pleasure, it crawls in pain. And on no one does its weight fall more heavily than on the soldier. Yet as the platoon wound carefully along the dusty road time warred with itself. It crawled when the men thought of their march, it ran insanely when they thought of their objective. Over them hung the fear and the threat that something was going to happen, that *Something* was going to happen. They did not feel that they could move fast enough to beat time to the punch. In a normal route march a man can let his faculties go dull, he can become numb. He can slog on, unaware of his surroundings, unaware of anything save the back of the man who slogs in front of him. But under fire, during a landing, during an advance, he must keep continuously on the alert. He must seek out rocks and trees and attempt to see through them. He must recognize that there is an enemy very near at hand and that even the landscape can rise up and kill him.

"Suppose this road is mined, Sergeant," Cousins said over his shoulder.

"Don't worry about it," Porter said.

"Okay," said Cousins. "Not till after."

In the second squad Privates Carraway and James were discussing music.

"That's one thing I want to do when I get back,"

Private Carraway said. "I want a nice collection of records."

"I knew a guy must of had millions of records," said Private James. "Millions, that guy had. He worked in the NBC studios. He had all kinds of autographs. You couldn't name anybody he didn't have an autograph. They even used to sign his records. He had a record of the Andrew Sisters with all three of their autographs. That's the kind of life."

"Just the music is all I want," Carraway said. "I got one collection, but I want a big one. I got all the Bing Crosby records except the last ones."

"You know Russ Columbo? My sister used to be nuts about Russ Columbo. She stayed in her room all the time the day he died."

"Too bad. When'd he die, anyway?"

"Hell, I don't know. Must of been ten years ago. She was a kid. She's married now."

"Her husband in the Army?"

"Beats me. I never heard from her."

"Maybe he's in a war plant."

"That's the life, the war plants. Two hundred bucks a week they drag down."

"The hell with the dough. I'd just like to be able to go home at night."

"If I hadn't gone in the Army I was going to California."

"Have a job there?"

"Naw, I just always wanted to go to California. Out with the movie stars."

"There was an old Crosby picture in Tunis. I hope nothing happened to those records."

Archimbeau felt resentful, though he couldn't quite tell why. As he walked he scuffed and kicked at dry clods of soil. He was carrying his rifle loosely in his right hand, carefully balanced between stock and barrel. As he advanced he kept turning his eyes from right to left and back again. He was angry at the terrain. It was all alike. Dry as dust. And when it wasn't dry as dust it was wet, and when it wasn't wet it was cold. But it all seemed to be the same country. From his left-hand pocket he took a stick of gum and held it with his hand while he tore away the paper with his teeth and pulled the long flat stick into his mouth. As he chewed it he thought of Trasker, and Trasker's jaw. Nothing to it. He never knew what hit him. A good guy. What had happened in that ravine was his fault. He had tripped Trasker in the dark. Trasker never knew. Meant to tell him. Always meant to tell him.

Allied planes were over the beaches, flying very high, back and forth. They would fly five miles toward the north, bank, and come back down again. Beneath them the shells were still exploding on the beach and in the water. They were dangerously near the platoon—really within ducking distance—but there was no time to be wasted dodging shells. There was no time to be wasted on anything. Ahead of the men, like an abyss, stretched the next two hours. But it was not a dark abyss, for the sun was shining very brightly.

As a matter of fact, it was out of that bright sun that the Focke-Wulf came at them.

# 5

THERE WAS so much noise that it was almost impossible to hear it. The planes to the south and the artillery fire and the occasional chatter of a machine-gun made hearing difficult. Archimbeau spotted the Focke-Wulf by instinct more than anything else. Ahead of him, in the sun, he caught an odd flash in the sky, a flash not of gold but silver. He did not even wait to ascertain exactly what it was. He threw up one hand, turned his head over his shoulder, yelled "Plane!" and made for the ditch.

Sergeant Porter blew his whistle, and the platoon broke for both sides of the road. Most of them made for the ditch. A few bolted for the open field on the other side of the road. As the men scattered the plane's machine-guns opened up. Two men who were making for the field seemed to trip clumsily and went tumbling down. The rest of the platoon made it.

The plane flashed past. It was a Focke-Wulf all right, a dirty scum of a double-tailed Focke-Wulf. Tyne saw the pilot wave his hand to them as he flashed past. He continued on down the road, banked to the north, and went after the beach. He had come in very low, the way the three Messerschmitts had, over the foothills. It was only by the grace of God that Archimbeau had seen anything. It was pure luck.

"Anybody hurt?" Sergeant Porter yelled up and down the ditch. "Anybody hurt?"

"All right down here," Tyne said.

Porter came scrambling down to where Tyne was crouched. "Did you see that?" he wanted to know. "Did you see that? Right out of the blasted sun. The dirty bastard."

"There's some wounded across the road," Tyne said. "My squad, I think. I'd better go over."

"Wait a minute. He may be back."

"I'll take my chances," said Tyne. He climbed out of the ditch and ran across the road. Five men were lying over there. "Who's hurt?" he said. One of the men was lying on his back. Tyne went over to him. It was Private Dugan, quite past hurting.

"Smitty got one," a man said.

"Get the hell over in that ditch," Tyne said. "Where's he got it?"

"Arm and shoulder."

"Give me a hand with him. Get the hell into the ditch."

Tyne and Private Phelps picked up Private Smith. The other two men ran across the road and leaped into the ditch. One of them picked up Dugan's rifle as he ran.

"He's out," Phelps said.

"Never mind." They brought Smith across the road

and lowered him into the ditch. "Dugan's dead," Tyne said to Porter.

"I know."

"Look at that Jerry," Private Friedman screamed. The Focke-Wulf was making an Immelmann to come back along the beach. It was just a speck in the sky, far to the north. Above it, almost leisurely, three Allied planes swung out of formation and went into a steep dive. The Focke-Wulf pilot didn't seem to see them. He dipped his nose and came back down toward the south. The three Allied planes, whatever they were, hit him all at once. He saw them too late and tried to pull his ship up in a steep climb. They got him while he was starting it. The Focke-Wulf seemed to nose straight up, stopped, hovered a bit, and then fell back down again, going into a spin and exploding as it hit the water. The three planes went into a graceful climb, on their way back to join the formation.

"Beautiful!" Friedman yelled. "Beautiful, beautiful."

"No more waving for that baby," Tyne said.

"Did he wave?" Porter asked.

"I saw him. Probably the bastard was grinning, too. Always leave them laughing."

Smith's wounds weren't serious, but they would be painful. The sulfa was out and was going on, but Smith would be out of action for quite a while. "What the hell can we do with him?" Porter asked. "Can we leave him here?"

Tyne looked up and down the road. "We'll have to," he said. "Can't take him with us."

"Nobody'll find him."

A frown of concentration appeared on Tyne's face. "The best thing we can do is wait till we get as far forward as we can, then send a man back. Things may be cleared up down here by then. The guy can bring back the stretcher-bearers. They can take care of Hoskins and Giorgio, too."

"Okay," Porter said. "You pick a man."

"There's no hurry."

"Think we'd better get on with it?"

"I'd wait awhile if I were you. There may be more where that came from." Tyne gestured down the road, where the Focke-Wulf had gone into its last spin. "Better take a ten, anyway."

"Tell 'em, will you?" Porter said.

Tyne walked down the ditch. "Take ten," he said over and over.

"Can I smoke, Corporal?" Rivera asked.

"Burn," Tyne said.

"Butt me, Friedman," said Rivera.


The dial on Tyne's watch told him they had been moving for twenty minutes, more or less. That meant a mile, roughly—a mile away from the beach and a mile away from the shells. Five miles to go to the farmhouse. Tyne was beginning to get worried about tanks. The Germans, in the time they had had, could have brought tanks all the way from Rome and played a few games of red dog on the route. Perhaps the enemy tanks had already arrived by another road and were joined where the machine-guns and small-arms fire could be heard. There must have been more roads leading from the beach, and more important roads into the bargain. Otherwise they would never have sent a single platoon to hold one road, especially at such a great distance from the point of landing. The whole thing, Tyne decided, would make a nice problem to mull over in his old age—if, as, and when. Surely the road they were on could not be of much importance. They must be getting the tanks ashore by now, and if the road had any value the tanks would be trundling themselves along it. It was almost certain that the tanks were aiming northeast. The platoon's job, in all probability, was to go to the farmhouse, blow the bridge, and thus make any counterattack impossible. That must be it, surely.

During the break many of the men were getting at their rations. Tyne began to feel hungry again. He opened a tin of cold hash and ate it with relish. He had not had much of it lately; it was only when a man ate it day after day and meal after meal that the hash became unbearable. Then one was just as apt to throw it away as eat it. The hash was, of course, supposed to be eaten warm; but whoever had put it up had neglected to include smokeless firewood, or firewood of any kind, or leisure. One ate rations only when one was in a hurry; otherwise the thing to do was scrounge. In Sicily it had been watermelons and neat, small tomatoes. Here there was (or seemed to be) nothing. Only brown grass and dry mud. Nothing palatable at all.

Rivera and Friedman, too, were eating hash, loudly and with the gusto of Socrates taking the hemlock.

75

"You know where they get this stuff?" Friedman asked.

"Yeah," said Rivera. "I know where they get everything."

"Where do they get this stuff?"

"You know the sewers?"

"What sewers?"

"Any sewers. The Hoboken sewers."

"How do you know? You got a brother works in the sewers?"

"Never mind my relations. You want me to tell you how they get it out of the sewers?"

"No. I'm eating it, for Christ's sake."

"We should be in the Heinie Army."

"They wouldn't take me," said Friedman. "Why should we be in the Heinie Army?"

"The god-damned food. It's good food."

"How the hell do you know? You a spy or something?"

"How about that HQ we walked into in Sicily? Wine on the table. Steak. A picture."

"It was Officers' Mess."

"So what? Do our Officers' Mess get wine on the table? Do they get steak? The Heinies are really eating."

"They won't be." Grimly.

"Listen, chum, in three years the whole world will be eating C rations. I got it from a friend."

"Give it back to him. I ain't interested."

"Don't you think of nothing but your gut? You're fat, Friedman. You're a chunk, Friedman."

"What the hell. First thing I'm going to do when I

get home is eat the god-damnedest biggest meal any guy ever ate. I wouldn't even tell you what I'm going to have. You're too insensitive."

"Butt me, Friedman."

"Listen, Rivera, all I been doing is feeding you fags. You think I bought out the American Tobacco Company or something?"

"Butt me."

"Ah, for Christ's sake."

"What do you get out of it, Friedman?"

"Out of what?"

"The business."

"What business?"

"This business."

"I ain't a member of the firm."

"You saw that Focke-Wulf."

"Yeah."

"He was after you."

"I wasn't in when he called."

"How about a match, for God's sake? There'll be another one right along. Any minute now."

"I won't be in then, either."

"Friedman, you're a draft dodger. You're yellow, Friedman."

"That's what I am, all right. Hold that match."

Sergeant Porter was crumbling a clod in his hand. He broke off a small piece of it, crumbled it in his palm, and then let the fine dirt sift through his calloused fingers. He counted the number of pieces he could break from each clod—good-sized pieces, about an inch through. From one clod he got seven; from another nine. There were no more good-sized clods near him. He did not feel like getting up to find one. He felt, as a matter of fact, bored and listless. Events seemed to have moved past and beyond him. Sergeant Porter was completely out of his depth. The dry hot plain stretched around him, full of an emptiness that gripped him around the throat and made him afraid. It was hard to say just what was the matter with Sergeant Porter.

Perhaps he had had too much war. Certainly he had had a lot of it—nearly a year. Scenes from Tunisia and Sicily kept flashing before his eyes. Men vary in the amount of war they can take. Some are good only for one action, others can stand it for years. But when a man gets enough of it, when he gets fed up, when he begins to tremble slightly and shift his eyes around or tremble slightly and stare eternally at one fixed spot, there is only one thing to do. Pull him out of the line and ship him back where the steak grows on trees and the only noise is that of the sunset gun. He may be some good there, but he'll be through in the line.

That was almost the way it was with Porter. He was a good man, but he had run his course. He had seen a lot of action and he had gone through it with his head down and his eyes open. But he had reached what amounted to the end of his rope. He wasn't beginning to tremble yet, but he was getting the shifty eye, the eye that doesn't know what is waiting behind the tree or on the other side of the deserted house. Any soldier is expected to have an eye like that, but when they reach the end of the tether the thing that is waiting on the other side of the tree or the other side of the house has become inhuman. It is no longer an enemy—living, breathing, capable of death—but it is *The* Enemy. And Porter was beginning to get get that feeling. It was growing on him day by day, it was keeping him awake at night. He was beginning to see things out of the corner of his eye.

Sergeant Porter was, as a matter of fact, ready for the cleaners. He was a good man, but he had reached the end of the tether. All that remained was for the tether to break.

"I've got a hell of a headache," Porter said to Tyne. The latter had come back from calling the break and was sitting beside his platoon commander. "A lousy headache."

"Tough," Tyne said.

"You trust this operation?"

"How do you mean?"

"You know. I don't like the ring of it. It doesn't ring true. There's something funny about it."

Tyne told him what he thought of it: that to blow up the bridge at the farmhouse meant protecting the flank, that a fast-moving small body of men could get through quicker than anything else and accomplish the mission.

"It sounds all right," Porter admitted. It seemed to Tyne that Porter had shriveled somehow. He didn't look as burly as he once had; he didn't even look as solid as he had early in the morning.

"It's the only thing," Tyne said solemnly. "As I see it," he added.

"Everything's been screwed up ever since we started," said Porter. "First we lose the lieutenant, then McWilliams, then Hoskins, then we get machine-gunned. It's all been bad."

"You've got to expect the machine-guns," Tyne said. He thought of McWilliams. There had been a lot like McWilliams. Smith was groaning a little, but he was smoking a cigarette at the same time, so it couldn't be too bad. Smith was out of it for a while. The groans just meant that he was working for his Purple Heart. There were many men in the Army who would be glad to be in Smith's shoes.

"I don't like the responsibility," Porter said. "It's not a sergeant's job. If I'd wanted the responsibility I'd have been an officer."

"You're stuck with it," Tyne said. He saw Porter's point, however. It was no joke, getting through to that farmhouse. Anything might happen. He was still worried about the tanks.

"Tanks," he said aloud.

"Huh?"

"I hope to God they don't send tanks along here before we get to that farmhouse."

"Jesus, you think they will?"

"You never know."

"We'd better get moving, hadn't we?"

"I think we had. If I were you I'd keep off the road. Let's take it along the ditch. It seems to follow the road pretty well; as far as we can see, anyway."

Porter considered for a moment. "Okay. What about Smith?"

"I'll talk to him."

With an effort Tyne rose to his feet and went over to where Smith was lying in the ditch, his pack underneath his head. "How you feeling, Smith?"

"In the pink, in the pink."

"Think you can stay here by yourself for a while?"

"Leave me some butts."

"Sure you'll be all right?"

A low groan. "Sure, Corporal; just leave me some butts."

"Someone will be coming to pick you up." Tyne took his pack of cigarettes from his pocket and gave it to Smith. It was nearly full. "He'll stay," he said to Porter when he went back.

"We'd better get started, then," Porter said.

He blew his whistle. Grumbling, the platoon rose to its feet.

Porter walked to the head of the column. "We'll stick to the ditch this time," he told them. "Keep the same formation, but stick to the ditch."

Casually the squads gathered together. Tyne took up his place as last man in the column. He listened to the sounds of battle to the north. They had increased perceptibly in volume. The battle sent its noises out in three sections. From far inland came the dull throb of enemy artillery, two or three miles inland from the beachhead was the sound of small arms, grenades, machine-guns and mortars, and from the sea came the thunder of the ships' guns. Added to this and forming a blanket for it was the hum of aircraft circling endlessly over the beach. Tyne imagined that it was wooded country where the small-arms fire could be heard; there must be a lot of sniping going on. That was the main engagement; there could be no doubt about it. The platoon was completely out of that phase of the action. He was convinced that their job was to prevent any flank attack, and he wondered incuriously if Porter had accepted his theory. The way Porter was acting, it looked like he would accept a theory that said the road they were on lead to Gettysburg, Pa.

Tyne started to reach for a cigarette, then realized that he had given all he had to Smith. He walked over to where Smith was lying in the ditch. "Can I bum one of those butts back, Smitty?" he asked.

"Help yourself, Corporal," Smith said. Then: "How long you think I'll be here?"

"Beats me," Tyne said. "It shouldn't be long, though. There'll be plenty of company coming up this road pretty soon."

"What company?"

Tyne grinned. "Any kind you want. Take it easy, Smitty."

He walked away. "If I want anything I'll ring," Smith called after him. He had forgotten to groan.

Up front Porter blew his whistle. The platoon started to move. They could make time along the ditch just as well as on the road; as a matter of fact, it was easier going, because it was level. There were no dry clods of mud and no ruts. They stepped out briskly. It could almost have been a route march. But every man's ears strained toward the thundering hell to the north, and every man's mind strained ahead of him. Tenseness was in every face. Uneasiness had pervaded the whole platoon; now none of them liked the situation. Each spine was possessed of an unnatural rigidity; they were all stiff and uneasy. They had begun to fear the road that ran along by the ditch. It had taken on proportions beyond any intentions of those who had once driven their carts and wagons over it. The road ran, a skinny, unsatisfactory ribbon, toward the crouching Unknown, the dangerous future. Over it at any time might appear a motorcyclist or an armored car or a tank. The next five miles were full of terrors.

Before them stretched a series of little hills, wooded in patches. They were getting away from the level ground that merged with the beaches. Somewhere in this district was a great plain, but they did not seem to be anywhere near it. Nowhere could they see any signs of life—either houses or fields or men. Only the ditch and the crude road proved that this was inhabited country. If it had not been for the sounds of battle a great and utter silence would have hung over that place.

Behind them three P-38's crossed the road, flying low, heading for the firing. Strafe job, Porter thought as he watched them pass and vanish over the low hills. He wished that three of them would roar up the road ahead of the platoon and see what was going on. But then, he decided, if anything was happening up there one of the planes would have noticed it. He felt slightly comforted by the number of Allied planes over the beach. It was obvious that they had air superiority, and that meant a lot. It could mean everything. It might even save them, though Porter could not say, even to himself, what it would save them from.

All he had was a half-formed idea that they were walking into trouble. He did not know why he felt that way; all that he knew was that he did. It was an emotion that could not be called fear, because Porter was not afraid, not in the strict sense of the word. It was merely that he had developed an extraordinary sense of suspicion, which in its way can be more paralyzing than fear.

Porter had at last reached the stage where he hated to do anything. He could no longer bring himself to move of his own accord; he had to have someone else urge him on. He was not, however, completely passive. On the contrary, he preferred to force the issue by asking the other man leading questions. What did he think should be done? Should such and such a thing be done in such and such a way? He could no longer put his brain to work; he had to have a middleman between his body and his mind.

The gunfire made Porter nervous. Irresistibly he found himself drawn to it. Gunfire was understandable, dire though it might be. It was identified with men and actual happenings; there was nothing secret about it. You could hear the shell coming, you could see the sniper in the tree, you could lie under the machine-gun's swath. But moving toward an unknown destination through secretive country was hard. Porter wished desperately that Halverson were not dead. Perhaps, he thought, he wasn't dead at all. There was no confirmation. McWilliams couldn't have seen him.

On a sudden impulse Porter dropped out of the column and waited until Tyne came abreast of him.

"What's the matter, Eddie?" Tyne asked.

"About Halverson," Porter said. "Did McWilliams see them bring him in?"

Tyne thought a moment. "No," he said slowly. "He said Tolliver told him."

"Who's Tolliver?"

"He's a guy in B Company."

"Never heard of him."

"He must have been a friend of McWilliams."

"Did he know Halverson?"

"He must have. He said he saw Halverson."

"And he said Halverson was dead?"

"That's what Mac said."

They walked on in silence for a minute.

"Bill," Porter said, "suppose Halverson isn't dead. Suppose this guy had him confused with somebody else. Suppose there was somebody who looked like him."

"Suppose there was."

"I don't think Halverson's dead, Bill. What do you think?"

"God damn it, I don't know. All I know is what Mac told me."

"I don't think he's dead, Bill."

"I hope he isn't. I don't wish any hard luck to anybody."

"Sure as hell, he's going to show up here. I'll bet you anything he's trying to catch up with us now. They can't knock off a competent bastard like Halverson. Guys like that come through every time."

Tyne studied Porter's face. "Do you want to stop and wait?" he asked. There was a suspicion of sarcasm in his voice.

"No, that wouldn't do any good," Porter said seriously. "I wish to hell he was here, though."

"Give me a cigarette," said Tyne. He took a deep mouthful of smoke as he watched Porter jog heavily back to the head of the little column.

Archimbeau was plotting the course of the war as he strode along. He was trying to improve on the fact that he expected to fight the Battle of Tibet eventually, and he was trying to remember geography that had slipped his mind in the eighth grade. There was, he was sure, a country east of Tibet, but he was goddamned if he could think of it. All he could think of was Afghanistan, and as he remembered it that was somewhere around India. Victor McLaglen in the movies was always fighting around there. He had the itinerary down pretty well up to Tibet, though. Archimbeau, who did not, in all seriousness, expect to see the shores of the United States for three years, wondered where he would have gone if he had been sent to a place like New Guinea. Probably to some of those islands and then to Burma or some place. He wished he had an atlas; first chance he had he'd get one.

"Hey, Cousins," he said. "What comes after Tibet?"

"What comes where after Tibet, for God's sake?"

"In the war. Where we going to fight the war after Tibet?"

"How the hell do I know? In bed."

"There's a country. I can't think of its name."

"There's a million countries I can't think of their names."

"All right, I just asked. Forget it."

But Cousins had suddenly lost interest in Archim-beau. Over on the left, about five hundred yards away, he saw two figures coming toward them.

"Arch," he said softly. "Look."

Archimbeau looked. And as he saw the figures Cousins turned and went running back to Sergeant Porter. He crouched a little as he ran.

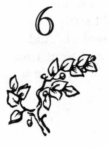

# 6

"WHAT THE hell are they?" Sergeant Porter asked.

"Damned if I know," Cousins said. "Too far away."

"Ward," Porter said. "Take a couple of men and go down and see."

"Johnson, Riddle," Ward said. The three of them cut away from the ditch, crossed the road, and moved over the field.

"Take it easy," Porter said after them.

Sergeant Ward had a grenade in his hand and his carbine crooked under his left arm. The figures had disappeared in a little gully. "Fan out a little," Ward said.

Johnson and Riddle fanned out as Ward broke into a trot. They picked up the pace from him. Suddenly Ward flung himself down on the ground; the privates followed him.

Two hundred yards away the figures appeared again. They were men, walking fast. Every ten seconds one of the men would look behind him as though he feared pursuit. They were Italian soldiers, evidently unarmed.

Ward rose to his feet and whistled at them. The looked in his direction and stopped dead in their tracks. One of them started to run. The other man said something to him, and he stopped uncertainly. Then he came back. Ward made a gesture for them to come to him. They hesitated for a moment and then, without a word passing between them, they simultaneously broke into a run.

Ward, as they came up to him, looked them over calmly. They looked dead beat. Both had three days' worth of beard and their uniforms were torn and dirty. One man had torn the leg of his pants, and through the hole Ward could see a blood-soaked bandage.

When they came within ten feet they stopped running, smiled, and burst out into loud exclamations, one man's words running into the other's. One of them was just a kid, not more than nineteen; the other, with the injured leg, was about thirty.

"You speak English?" Ward asked the older man.

They both shook their heads violently in the affirmative and went on talking Italian.

"Oh, hell," Ward said. He gestured for the men to follow him and started back toward the platoon. Johnson and Riddle fell in silently behind the Italians.

"Couple of wops," Ward said to Porter as he came up to the ditch.

"Yeah," Porter said. "They speak English?"

"Damned if I know."

"We'll find out," Porter said. "Hey, Giorgio!"

"Giorgio got wounded," Archimbeau said.

"What's the matter with me?" Porter said. "Yeah. Tranella!"

Tranella, a dark little man from Ward's squad, came over. "You want me, Sarge?" he asked.

"Can you talk Italian?"

"Sure I can talk Italian."

"Talk to these guys."

"What'll I say?"

"Ask them where they come from, for Christ's sake."

The two Italians were standing awkwardly, still grinning at nothing. Tranella looked calmly at them. "Where are you from?" he asked in Italian.

The two men gave loud exclamations of joy. The elder came over to Tranella and clasped him around the shoulders. *"Un compatriotto!"* he said.

"All right," Tranella said. "Where are you from?"

"Turin," the man said eagerly.

"He says he's from Turin," Tranella said to Sergeant Porter.

"Where's that, for God's sake?"

"Up north. 'Way up north."

"I don't mean that. Find out where he's coming from now."

"Oh. Where are you coming from?"

The Italian waved his hands toward the north. "There is a battle up there," he said. "We are running away from the battle. Before that we were running away from the Germans. We are no longer fighting."

Tranella translated.

"Ask him what's going on up there."

"What did you see of the battle?"

"Ah, we saw much of the battle. We were lying along the road and we saw the tanks go by. We heard the firing."

"What tanks?"

"The German tanks."

"He says they were lying along a road and they saw the Germans bringing up some tanks."

"Did the tanks go back again?"

"No, they did not go back again."

"One went off in a field," the younger man said.

"Yes," said the older man, "one went off in a field. It was one of the big ones, the Tigers."

"In which direction did the Tiger go?"

"Toward the sea," the older Italian said.

"Going toward the beach, Sergeant."

Porter looked back, along the road they had come. "When was this?"

"When was this?" Tranella translated.

"One hour ago," the man said. "Two hours ago. I have no watch. Neither of us has a watch."

"He doesn't know for sure. A couple of hours ago, maybe less."

"Ask him if he saw any Germans."

"Did you see any *tedeschi?*"

"I saw only the tanks. But there are many roads up there. There are many roads the *tedeschi* could use."

"Only the tanks, Sergeant."

"God damn it, Tranella, see what you can find out. Ask him some questions."

"I am, Sergeant."

"Well, find out something."

"Ask him if he knows this country," Tyne said.

"The corporal wants to know if you know this country."

The older Italian smiled at Tyne. "I am from the north, but I know this country. I was once stationed here. I have maneuvered in this area."

"He says yes."

"Good," Tyne said. "Where's the map, Eddie?"

"What map? Oh. It's here." Porter passed him the map case.

"We have here," Tyne said as he unfolded it, "a map of the area. Tell him that, Tranella."

Tranella told him. The Italian nodded vigorously. "I too am a corporal," he said. "I have handled maps."

Tyne spread the map out on the brown grass, where it developed pointed little hills of its own at the folds. "We are here, I think," he said, putting a dirty finger at a point along the road. "Ask him if I am right?"

"Are we where the corporal has put his finger?"

The older Italian fell on his knees beside Tyne and the younger one crowded over his shoulder. "Yes," he said, "we are there. Perhaps a little farther on. There is where the battle is." He pointed to a road junction at the far left of the map. "And here is where we saw the tanks."

"Is it bad country?" Porter asked.

"The sergeant wants to know if it is bad country."

"It is good country for defence. We have defended it up there in the maneuvers. It is rough. There are many ravines. The rain makes them. This road will take you to country like it."

"It is very dusty," the young man said.

"Have the Germans many men there?" Tranella wanted to know.

"Who knows?" said the older Italian. "Who knows about the *tedeschi?* They have beaten us. Everyone has beaten us. We are no longer soldiers."

"He says he don't know how many Germans are around," Tranella said.

"There were many *tedeschi* in this place," the Italian said, pointing to a town. "But that was five months ago. Who knows now?"

"The Germans are everywhere," the younger man said. "I myself have killed *un tedesco.*"

"This young guy says he's knocked off a Kraut," Tranella said.

"Ask him where," said Porter.

"Where'd you kill the German?"

"I killed him in Capua. I hit him with a rock."

"We have left the Army," the older Italian said. "We are going south. He has relatives down there."

"An uncle," the young man said.

"We have to hide sometimes," the older said. "I think the Germans would kill us if they found us. I did not want this war."

"Nor I," the young man said.

"Things are different in the north," said the older.

"My people are from Milan," Tranella said. "They have told me about it there."

"Then you know what things are like there," said the Italian. "We are working people. We did not want war. We did not want the Germans. They give you no choice. Now we can not go home. The Germans cover the north like beetles."

"They won't," Tranella said.

The older man shrugged. "It is hard to say. They are very difficult."

"He's griping about the Germans," Tranella said.

"For God's sake," said Porter, "do you think we've got nothing to do but sit around while he tells us what's the matter with Italy? We know what's the matter with Italy. Find the hell out about that farmhouse."

"This farmhouse here," Tyne said. "Ask him if he knows anything about it."

Tranella pointed to the house on the map. "Do you know anything about this farm?"

The Italian studied the map carefully. "I don't know," he said. "It is hard to say. This is not one of our maps. Yes, I remember that place. I remember that bridge. That is a nice farm."

"Ask him what kind of bridge it is."

"What kind of bridge is it?"

The Italian looked puzzled. "That I do not remember. It may be wood. It may be steel. It may be concrete. There are so many bridges."

"He don't know," Tranella said.

"Ask him does he know where I can get a pizza," Rivera said.

"Shut up," said Sergeant Porter.

"I can tell you one thing," the Italian said. "Inland there are many *tedeschi*."

"He says there 're a lot of Krauts a few miles along," Tranella said.

"How many?"

"Who can tell? Everywhere there are many."

"He says he hasn't got any god-damned idea."

"I would like a cigarette," the older Italian said.

"I, too," said the younger.

"Now they both want butts," Tranella said.

"Give them a couple," Porter said.

"Out of my own, for God's sake?" Tranella said.

"Give them a couple," Tyne said.

Tranella gave each of the Italians a cigarette and lit them for them. They inhaled deeply and luxuriously.

"Good," said the younger. "Good tobacco."

"The best," said the older. "Well," he said to Tranella, "now we are your prisoners. We shall follow you."

"He says they're our prisoners and that they're going to come along," Tranella said.

"The hell they are," Porter said. "We aren't at war with Italy any more. They can go where they goddamn please."

"You can go," Tranella said.

The older man gave a gesture of surprise. "But where can we go?" he asked. "We have no money. The Germans will get us."

"They're your friends," Tranella said.

"We are hungry, too," said the older Italian.

"Now the bastards say they're hungry," Tranella said.

"Give them some K ration," Porter said.

"They can take this," Rivera said. He tossed a can of K ration to the older Italian. "When they get a mouthful of that crap they'll wish Italy never went out of the war. They'll think twice about the Americans next time."

"Tell them they will be safe here," Porter said.

"The sergeant says that you will be safe here," Tranella said. "No Germans will come here."

"We would rather go with you," the older Italian said.

"It is an order," said Tranella. Then, to Porter: "God-damnedest people I ever saw."

"We might as well go on," Porter said to Tyne.

Tyne carefully folded the map and put it back in the case. "We might as well," he said.

"Thanks, Tranella," Porter said.

"Any time, Sarge." Tranella wandered back toward the rear of the little column. The Italians remained standing where they were, confused and uneasy.

"We don't know any more than we did before," Tyne said. "Not a damned bit more."

"Did you expect to?" Porter wanted to know.

"They might have known something."

"They never know anything. I've seen too many of them come in. They know all about the private lives of their god-damned lieutenants, but they don't know anything else. They never know anything else. You always draw a blank."

Porter blew his whistle and the column started off again. "Stay up here with me, Bill," he said. "I want to talk to you."

The Italians stood watching the platoon pass them. They were still watching as the last men disappeared over the crest of a small hill. The older one still had the can of K ration clutched in one hand.

"That's the Italians for you," Rivera said.

"What's the Italians?" Friedman wanted to know.

"All give and no take."

"What nationality are you, Rivera?"

"I'm a god-damned Irishman. What did you think I was?"

"I was just wondering, that's all."

"So help me God, I hope I never see another Italian after this war. I never want to see another one. My God, in Tunisia they were even surrendering to generals."

"How many surrendered to you?"

"All the ones that surrendered to me were dead. A guy in my position never sees any live ones."

"You're a tough baby, Rivera."

"I sure as hell am."

"What are you going to do after the war?"

"Join a mob. I'm a mobster."

"What did you do before the war?"

"Friedman, sixty million times you asked me that. I was an undertaker. I undertook stiffs."

"How'd you like the job?"

"It made my hands smell."

"Why don't you join the Graves Registration Squad of the QMC? That's right up your alley."

"I can't spell, for God's sake. Judson, you look like a bright boy. Why don't you join the Graves Registration Squad of the QMC?"

"How's the pay?" Judson asked.

"Lousy."

"Is there any future in it?"

"What the hell do you care about the future?" Friedman said. "You ain't even living in the present."

"That's right, Jakie," said Rivera. "You're a smart apple, Jakie. A character reader. A reader of character."

97

"What do you mean I ain't living in the present?" Judson demanded.

"I'll ask you," Friedman said. "Where are you now?"

"Italy."

"How do you know you're in Italy? You seen any signposts in Italian?"

"We landed in Italy."

"How the hell you know you landed in Italy? Just because somebody told you? You believe all you hear?"

"I just seen a couple of Italians."

"In Tunisia," Rivera said, "you seen a million Italians. Was that Italy? Naw, it was Tunisia. You're ignorant, Judson."

"All right," Judson said, "if we ain't in Italy, where are we?"

"Sunny France," Friedman said. "Marching up to Armentières. Where the hell did you think we was?"

"Italy," said Private Judson stubbornly.

"I give up," Friedman said.

"So do I," said Rivera. "If the privates are dumb, Jesus, think what the generals must be like. I'm going to get out of this Army."

"Me, too," Friedman said. "Move over."

In the second squad Privates James and Carraway were discussing Art.

"The *Saturday Evening Post* has the best covers," James said. "That guy. What's his name? Norman Rockwell. He can draw covers to beat all hell. He had some covers about the Army."

"I'll take a camera picture any day," said Carraway. "Drawing's okay, but it ain't real. I like things to be real."

"Jesus, this guy Rockwell made it look just like a picture. I used to look at them. It looks just like a picture, I used to say. You'd never of known it was painted."

"He should of took a picture and saved time."

"Ah, you can't get the touch in a picture," James said.

"Drawings was all right when they didn't have cameras," said Carraway. "But now they got cameras, so you don't have to draw."

"That's screwy."

"Why is it screwy?"

"You might just as well say that now they got moving pictures so there's no sense in taking regular pictures. You might just as well have a movie on the cover of a magazine."

"Someday they'll have it, maybe."

"Naw, they won't. Maybe they'll have movies that'll smell, though. Maybe the scene will be in a garden or something and you can smell the flowers."

"I'd like to see one of them laid in a brewery right now," Carraway said, "so I could smell the beer. If a guy came along right now and said, 'What'll you give me for a can of Ruppert's?' I'd give him my god-damned rifle and my god-damned bayonet and even my god-damned pants."

"You don't need pants in this climate, anyway. Except at night."

"The British got the right idea. They ought to issue us some of these short pants, too."

"These uniforms is the worst I ever ran into."

"You never ran into any others."

"When I come into the Army they were issuing blue fatigues. That's how long I been in the Army."

"When I come into the Army they were issuing muzzle-loading rifles. That's how long *I* been in the Army."

Sergeant Porter and Corporal Tyne slogged along in silence. Porter kept his head down, as though he were studying the ground before his feet. Tyne kept his eyes straight ahead, watching the backs of the scouts, Cousins and Archimbeau. Occasionally he looked sidewise at Porter. The thought of the two Italians kept running through his head.

He knew very little about Italy, but when he considered it he imagined that he probably knew as much about it as he did any other country, excepting his own. Italy, England, France, and Germany—those were the countries Americans knew best. Tyne did not hate Italy, nor did he hate the Italians. He merely ignored them. Some of the men, he knew, hated them—not necessarily because they had killed their share of Americans, but because they were cowards. They ran. They always ran. A soldier could hate the Germans, but he would respect them at the same time. He would respect their stubborn bravery and their cunning and their battle wisdom. But the Italians had none of these negative virtues. The Italians had nothing.

The two ex-soldiers had, in a way, been pitiful.

They had been cast out on a world that they could no longer comprehend. And yet it had been a world they had helped to make, a world they had probably wanted to make, a world of confusion in which they and millions like them would have been the only elements possessed of power and will, or at least possessed of leaders who were possessed of power and will. But now the leaders were gone and the power and the will with them. What remained was chaos and ashes, a country shattered and a people lost.

"Bill," Sergeant Porter said, "did you ever have the feeling that something was going to happen to you?"

"I have it all the time."

"I've got it now."

"Don't worry about it."

"But I've never had it before. I don't like it. Something's happened to me."

"What?"

"I don't know. Look: if you have to, will you take over?"

"What about Ward?"

"I want you."

"Sure, Eddie. But don't worry so damned much. Everything's going to be all right."

"Everything's always all right," Porter said. He went back to staring at the ground.

He was beginning to frighten Tyne a little. Something was evidently the matter with Porter. It was as though he were in a vacuum, as though someone had put him in some great bottle and then had drawn out all the air. Porter was lifeless, limp. He seemed unable to form an opinion any more. Tyne rapidly ran through the places where he had seen Porter in action, where he had been most intimate with him. The places framed themselves like signposts in his mind—Tebessa, Gafsa, Bizerte, Gela, the hills of Sicily, and now here. There was a definite change in the man, a definite and dangerous change.

"Ward might not like anything like that," he said. He was trying to draw Porter out.

"Why shouldn't Ward like it?" Porter demanded. He did not raise his eyes from the ground. "There's no reason why he shouldn't like it. He has his job."

"We all have our jobs," Tyne said.

Said Sergeant Porter, "I don't feel well. I feel goddamned lousy. My head aches."

The ditch stopped abruptly, for no apparent reason. They were coming into lightly wooded country, of rather sharper slopes. Here and there a great boulder could be seen. The trees looked ancient and gnarled. None of them were very large; it was as though they could not draw enough sustenance from the soil and were sentenced to be forever stunted. There was an air of strain about the trees, as though they were striving to increase themselves, to swell in size, under impossible and unreasonable conditions.

When the ditch stopped, Archimbeau swerved over to the road without awaiting any command. The rest of the column trailed after him. As far as Archimbeau was concerned they might just as well walk on the road as anywhere else. It made no difference to him. It was all the same country, all the same war. The same dangers were everywhere. He did not expect any more planes to come over. Allied planes were covering the territory pretty well; they were passing over the column frequently now, and if anything went wrong, either on the road ahead or around them, the planes would spot it. As far as Archimbeau was concerned the operation had developed into an automatic business. All they had to do was get to where they were going, do what they had to do, and then relax. It was simple; it was as simple as anything ever was. It was as simple as the Battle of Tibet would be. That was always the way it was in the Army. Things looked complicated as hell, but when you came to do them they were simple. Archimbeau thought of Trasker—the suddenly stilled voice, the smashed jaw, the bereft body. Death was like that.

"Cousins," he said, "you married?"

"Naw," Cousins said. "Why the hell should I be married?"

"After the war I'm going to get married."

"Okay. Go ahead."

"Honest to God, if I had a wife now she'd be sending me things. Cookies, maybe. Maybe a sweater. I haven't got a package since I come overseas."

"I haven't got a package either," Cousins said. "What the hell good is it anyway? You open it and you got to give something to everybody you know. There's no percentage in that. I'm just as happy. If I was married I'd have to be sending money home all the time, too. And God knows what my wife might be doing. The hell with it."

"When I get to Tibet," Archimbeau said solemnly, "I'm going to marry a Tibet woman."

"Okay," Cousins said. "Go ahead."

Time stopped in the sound of the moving feet. The clocks ran out. The sun stood still. The world contracted. To the north the battle, the battle that had not yet touched them, went on. They were a part of it and yet not a part of it. For the moment they were still individuals, because their group was small enough for them to be individuals. They had not yet become part of a huge and heaving mass. Each man was recognizable as himself. The platoon was part of a larger pattern, but it had not yet lost its identity. The battle whose noises rolled over the little hills at them was still standing and watching them go about their essential business; it had not yet beckoned them to come. They had been in an enemy country for five hours, and they had not yet seen an enemy.

# 7

THEY COULD hear the motorcycle coming over and above all other noises. Singly and in pairs they turned to look at it. None of them considered the possibility that it might be an enemy motorcycle; it was coming from the direction in which they had come, and it had to be one of theirs. It came slowly for a motorcycle. The rider was obviously having trouble with the rutty road. He jazzed his motor, modulated it, and then jazzed it again. Over the sound of the motorcycle they could hear Porter's whistle demanding that they halt. They halted, raggedly.

The rider bounced up to the head of the column and stopped by Sergeant Porter. He cut his motor. He was a sergeant, too.

"What's cooking, Jack?" he said to Porter.

"All quiet so far," Porter said. "Where you from?"

The rider ignored the question. "What's up this road?" he wanted to know.

"Damned if I know," Porter said. "Where you from?"

"I'm looking for the 25th. You seen the 25th anywhere?"

"The 25th what, for God's sake?"

"Infantry."

"Never heard of them."

The rider looked puzzled. "They were supposed to be up this road," he said.

"Anything can be up this road," Porter said.

"There are some other roads running from the beach," said Tyne. "They run right through the battle area, according to the map."

"Jesus," the rider said, "I didn't know there were any other roads. They just told me to go up the road. They didn't say anything about more than one. What the hell, that's the Army." He lit a cigarette.

"What's it like on the beach?" Porter asked.

"Okay," the rider said. "A little rough. They're shelling the god-damned place. Was that your man I saw down the road?"

"What man?" Porter asked.

"A little guy with a smashed-up shoulder."

"Yeah, he's ours. He all right?"

"Damned if I know. I just saw him sitting in a ditch. He didn't complain."

"Did you see a couple of Italian soldiers?" Porter asked.

"Christ's sake, they still fighting?" the rider asked.

"No, we just ran into them down the road."

"Didn't see them. What're you looking for up here, anyway?"

"Objective's a farmhouse," Porter said. "About three miles up the road."

"Anything up there?" the rider asked.

"Damned if I know."

"Want me to take a run up and see?"

"I thought you were looking for the 25th," Tyne said.

"They'll keep," said the rider. "It's not important. Nothing's important in this god-damned war."

"It'll be damned nice if you'll scout a couple of miles," Porter said. "Take a lot off my mind, anyway."

"Okay," the rider said. He flipped away his cigarette. "This is the first time I've been to Italy. I got to see the country."

He shoved his machine in gear and roared away up the road, vanishing over the brow of a hill. The platoon resumed its march.

"I feel better," Porter said. "Maybe I should have told him it was the farmhouse by the bridge. You think I should have told him that, Bill?"

"It's the only farmhouse there is," Tyne said. "He can't miss it."

"You can always miss," Porter said. "But I feel better. If the road's clear it might be all right after all. How long do you think it will take him to get back?"

Tyne considered. "Fifteen or twenty minutes," he said.

"That's the kind of a job to have," Friedman said. "A nice shiny motorcycle and a nice shiny carbine. No walking. Solid comfort."

"Between you and me, Jakie," said Rivera, "motorcycles scare hell out of me."

"I didn't think you were scared of anything."

"Women and motorcycles, Jakie. A butt."

Wearily Friedman passed him a cigarette and a match. "When I run out of butts," he said, "you'll be in a hell of a mess."

"I'll find a new friend," Rivera said.

"I'd still like to be sitting in his boots," said Friedman.

"Whose boots?"

"The guy on the motorcycle. It's a life."

"What are you, Friedman, a lousy hero?"

"I like my comfort."

"Those guys are dead pigeons. High mortality rate."

"So what?"

"That was the first sergeant I ever saw on a motorcycle. Most of them are lucky if they live to make corporal."

"Do you think you'll ever live to make corporal?"

"Baby, I just want to live long enough to make civilian."

"You've got no imagination, Rivera. You're a lump."

"Okay."

Sergeant Ward was thinking of apples. He didn't know why; he just happened to be thinking of apples. They made a wonderful picture in his mind—huge, red, and juicy. He thought of the different varieties, Baldwins, McIntosh Reds, pippins, russets. He imagined he was cutting one with a knife, the creamy flesh showing wet as he opened the halves. And the funny thing about it was that Ward didn't like apples very much. Occasionally he would eat one, but he wasn't one who went overboard for them. He'd take a pear any day. But right now it was apples. Pears were yellow and the country was yellow; the combination was bad. But apples were red and wet and cold and juicy. Sergeant Ward could feel the sweat oozing through his woolen shirt; the damp cloth clung to his back. It had seemed hardly warm enough last night, and now it was killing him. Stupid. Apples.

There were more trees, and from the crests of the little hills gaunt, rain-formed gullies cut down to the hollows. Incipient serious erosion was everywhere. With his practised farmer's eye Sergeant Ward studied the soil. He did not like it. It looked old and tired and worn out. Soil was like a body. If you didn't take care of it it would die. There was too much dead soil in the world. For nearly a year Sergeant Ward had been studying the earth. Most of what he had seen had been bad. There were some rich places in Tunisia. They took care of it there; they had taken care of it for centuries. Those were the people who really grew things, who wanted to grow things, who made things live for them. The soil in this small part of Italy was dry and barren and lifeless. Perhaps too many soldiers had walked on it. They had been walking on it for many, many years.

Sergeant Ward was a farmer, and he was also a man of strong opinions that, once formed, were changed only by an Act of God or his wife. He had nearly formed the opinion that Italy was a barren country. He could do it on just what he had seen since he had landed. And though he might spend the rest of his sojourn in Italy walking around in lush gardens and vineyards, he would never change his opinion. He would take it back to Vermont with him. He would spread it wherever he went. Sergeant Ward was not one to take the long view.

"It's time that rider was coming back," Porter said.

Tyne looked at his watch. "He's only been gone ten minutes."

"It seems longer."

"Take it easy, Eddie. It's a long war."

"I know. But everything takes so damned long. Nothing ever happens when it should happen."

"We're doing all right, Eddie."

He was not, of course, sure that they were doing all right. He wasn't sure of anything of the kind. On the contrary, he was worried about the whole business. Not in the way Porter was, though. Porter was more than worried: he was rattled. But Tyne had the natural worries of a careful man. He knew that it was possible for things to go smoothly, but the wisest thing was to take it for granted that they wouldn't. You couldn't go wrong that way. Then, if they turned out to be smooth after all, you felt so much the better. It was not the best philosophy in the world, but it worked.

"It's taking him a long time," Porter said.

"Take it easy, Eddie," Tyne said again.

"It's always the same," Porter said. "Nothing ever happens right. It's always been that way. It always will be that way. You wait for someone and he never shows up. You tell somebody to do somthing and he does it wrong. It's never going to be any different. Never. They put me on to this job, and I didn't want it. It isn't my responsibility. I don't understand this war. Everything's crazy. Nothing's gone right today. It's not going to get any better." He spoke in a flat, taut monotone that did not carry beyond Tyne's ears.

"You're worrying too much, Eddie," Tyne said soothingly. "There's nothing to worry about. It'll go along. It was worse in other places."

"In other places we knew where we were going," Porter said.

"Sometimes we didn't."

"We thought we did."

"This is a tough road. That rider can't make any time."

"They can always make time if they want to make time. Bill, I'm scared of the tanks."

"Why?"

"If they catch us on this road they've got us cold. Like mackerel."

The same idea had passed through Tyne's mind and had worried him. It was perfectly true; they'd be duck soup for tanks. Even one tank, for that matter. It could come up over one of the hills and be on them before they'd have time to scatter. And all they had was grenades and damned little cover. Tyne didn't relish the thought of the tanks. "There probably isn't a tank within five miles of here," he said. "They're all over where the noise is."

Porter stared at the ground. He did not answer.

"I wrote a letter to my wife," Private Johnson said to Private Riddle.

"All right," Riddle said.

"I wrote it in the landing barge. Hard as hell to write something when you can't see it."

"Why didn't you wait till daylight?"

"You never can tell," Johnson said. "A man doesn't want to take no chances. I even wrote the envelope in the dark. It looked good."

"How the hell do you know it looked good?"

"I saw it in the daylight. Then I give it to Sergeant Hoskins."

"What for, for Jesus' sake?"

"To mail for me."

"That old bastard'll probably tear it open and read it. He's probably reading it right now," Riddle said.

"Aw, he wouldn't do a thing like that."

"You never know what a sergeant will do. They do some god-damned funny things."

"He wouldn't do that."

"How do you know he wouldn't? Maybe he thinks there's money in it. Maybe he's using it for a bandage. He's got a bullet hole in him. Maybe he stuffed it in the bullet hole."

"You're crazy. You can't stuff paper in a bullet hole."

"How do you know you can't?"

"It crinkles."

"Jesus, what a dope. The next time you get a bullet hole in you, stuff some paper in it and see how it feels. Then you'll know."

"I never had a bullet hole in me."

"Wait'll you get one, then."

"Cut that stuff out, Riddle," Sergeant Ward said. "If he mailed a letter, he mailed a letter. Leave him alone."

"I was just kidding, Sarge," Riddle said.

"You got a mean streak, Riddle. Somebody's going to paste you one of these days."

"I'll wait," said Riddle. "Okay, Johnson, you mailed your letter." Then, in a whisper: "But you never know what sergeants will do."

"They won't do anything," Johnson said.

The battle seemed to be increasing. More artillery could be heard on both sides. The guns sounded deeper and more dangerous. The platoon was now far from the danger area. It was as though the country had taken the men in and hidden them. They were surrounded by a near silence, over which the noise of the battle seemed faint, foreign, and far away, as though it were coming to them over water, as though it were not their quarrel. It was the road that might betray them to the war. It was the one way out of the silence, their one link with the outside world. Over it the rider had gone, vanishing from what they knew into what they did not know. Impatiently they waited for his return. They did not talk to each other about it; rather the feeling was understood. The most important thoughts never have to be spoken.

The rider was late. He was overdue. They strained to catch the sound of his motor, roaring toward them out of the unknown country before them. Over their heads the trees reached out, trying to touch each other across the road. The trees were larger now, and of a different variety. Their branches were clean and lithe, but their trunks were warped and gnarled, as though they had had hard births. The whole country looked as though it had fought to come alive; either that or had lived too long. They all thought that, though none of them could have put it into words. With an instinct like that of animals, they could be satisfied or dissatisfied with a landscape on sight. They could see the whole thing as one great panorama, with everything in its place, without knowing what it was about the view that they disliked.

"I suppose you still think he'll be back," Porter said.

"He may have gone further on than we thought he would," Tyne said. "Or he might have got a flat."

"He didn't go too far and he didn't get a flat," Porter said. "He ran into trouble. Did you hear any firing?"

"Didn't hear a damned thing."

"He ran into trouble."

Exasperation surged up in Tyne. "For Christ's sake, Eddie," he said, "I don't know what's the matter with you or what you're thinking, but you're going to have everyone with their tongues hanging out if you don't snap out of it. What the hell's the matter?"

"I don't know." Porter brushed his hand across his forehead under the helmet. "My head aches."

"Are you sick?"

"I don't know. Leave me alone."

"Okay."

"Still want to be on a motorcycle, Ugly?" Rivera asked.

"Sure," Friedman said. "It's a life."

"In that guy's case, the question is—is it a life?"

"He's probably sitting under a tree somewhere, reading a book."

"Friedman, it's optimists like you that cause all

the trouble in the world. Where would he get a book?"

"How the hell do I know where he'd get a book?" Friedman took out a package of cigarettes, removed one, crumpled the package, and threw it away. "I'll let you watch me," he said.

"Open another god-damned pack," Rivera said.

"All I got, baby."

"A drag, then."

"I'll consider it."

"What's the point of having a motorcycle if they knock you off every time you get on to it? And if they don't knock you off you smack into a wall in the dark and knock yourself off. What's the point? Where's the percentage?"

"It's all in how you look at it," Friedman said. "A motorcycle is a civilized way to travel."

"We ain't in civilization," Rivera said. "We ain't anywhere. A drag."

Sighing, Friedman passed over his last cigarette. Rivera took a deep pull at it. "Take it easy," Friedman said. "Take it easy."

"I'm a hard man," said Rivera.

Time moved on to the sound of boots on earth. The minutes drummed by. As they passed Tyne realized that the rider would not be back, that he might never be back. In the time that had been allotted to him he could have gone to the farmhouse and a couple of miles beyond. Probably the platoon would never know what had happened to him. He might have found a road that turned off, though there was no road marked on the map. Perhaps he had run into trouble beyond the bridge near the farmhouse, for beyond that bridge the road forked, and the Germans always were hell on crossroads.

It was odd, Tyne thought, how many people you met in the Army who crossed your path for perhaps only a few seconds and then went on, never to be seen again. He could remember countless occasions and countless faces and countless voices. You never forgot the faces. In peacetime you could go into a store and talk to a clerk, but by the time you had left the store you had completely forgotten the clerk's face. It was different in war. You might see a man's face in the flash of an exploding shell or in the cab of a truck or peering out of a slit trench, and though you had never seen the face before and never would see it again, you couldn't forget it. War left impressions of unbelievable sharpness. It was almost as though men, in losing identity, gained identity. Their faces and voices became intense. They clung to the mind. They were like the hands of drowning men, reaching out of the water, refusing until the end to be devoured.

"Take a break," Porter said. "Tell them to take a break." Abruptly, without blowing his whistle, he turned off the road and strode in among the trees.

Tyne turned back to the column and held up his hand. "Take a break," he said in a loud, clear voice. "Take a break," he called ahead to the scouts.

The platoon moved off the road and into the trees. "Keep well back from the road," Tyne said. He did not want to take any chances of something coming along and nailing them. "Archimbeau, you stay out close to the road. If you see that rider coming back, wave to him." This last was for Porter's benefit.

Mumbling, Archimbeau walked back and settled down behind a bush close to the road. He had made up his mind that every dirty job in the Army was his personal property. He never missed. In the early days when they had wanted another KP it had always been Archimbeau who had been chosen. He had pulled guard more than anyone else in the outfit. He was always at the head of the column, where it hurt. And he was always crawling off on his belly somewhere. Sometimes Archimbeau wondered if he could stand it until the Battle of Tibet. That was a long time to hang on. He thought sadly of a set of corporal's stripes. In a decent outfit a guy who'd done all the work he had would be a corporal easy. Even a sergeant, with luck. But it was just like this lousy outfit to leave you hanging around for years with nothing to show for it but calluses and bunions. A lousy outfit like this never even got around to replacing officers. Too god-damned economical. Solemnly Archimbeau spat into the bush, directly in front of his eyes. He decided he didn't like Italy any better than he liked any place else. They could have it. He'd had it already.

Tyne went over to where Porter was sitting under a tree, his head in his hands. He sat down beside him.

"Feel bad, Eddie?" he asked.

Porter raised his face from his hands. "Lousy," he said. "I don't know what the hell's the matter with me. I never felt like this before."

His hands were shaking slightly as though he had a

117

fever. Tyne noted the fact and pursed his lips. "Maybe you'd better not go on," he said.

"Oh, hell, I've got to," said Porter. "They gave me this job and I've got to do it. It'll be all right."

"We'll get through," Tyne said. His voice carried as much conviction as he could manage. For the last half hour he had been getting that old Lost Patrol feeling, though there was really no reason for him to have it. The platoon was anything but lost. They knew where they were, and even if they didn't they could damned well find out by going toward the sound of the guns. Listening to the artillery, he noted that the fight was keeping within what seemed to be almost like defined boundaries. It did not appear to be spreading at all. It was odd that there were no flank movements of any kind. Or was he, himself, part of a flank movement? The Lost Patrol feeling he blamed on Porter. He was the one who was doing all the worrying. Everyone else was keeping his head. He suddenly felt very angry at Porter. When he said something like "We'll get through" he felt like a damned fool. This wasn't the movies.

"Something's up with the sergeant," Rivera said. He was lying on his stomach with his helmet off. His black hair was soaked and curly with sweat.

"Which sergeant?" Friedman asked.

"Porter."

Private Cousins was lying with them. "I noticed it," he said.

"Nobody tells me nothing," Friedman said.

"Keep your eyes open," said Rivera. "If you weren't smoking your last butts all the time and getting smoke in your eyes you might know more about what's going on."

"What's the matter with Porter?"

"How the hell do I know? I ain't a doctor. He's just acting funny, that's all."

"Working for a CDD," Cousins said.

"I'm a Section 8 man myself," Friedman said.

"You said it, honey," Rivera said. "Any time you want a certificate signed, just tap me on the shoulder."

"With an ax," Friedman said.

"The sergeant's been acting funny all day," Cousins said.

"This is a hell of a platoon," Rivera said. "In one morning we've lost one lieutenant and two non-coms, and have got another non-com feeling lousy. This platoon is hell on non-coms."

"Now I know why they want me to keep on being a private," Friedman said. "They want to spare me from grief."

"That sure as hell is the reason," Rivera said. "You can't say they ain't thoughtful."

Sergeant Ward came over and sat down by Porter and Tyne. "What's the matter, Porter?" he asked. "Feeling bad?"

"He feels lousy," Tyne said.

Porter had put his head back in his hands. He did not look up when Ward spoke.

"What's the matter?" Porter wanted to know.

Tyne shrugged.

"A guy can pick up anything in this kind of country," Ward said philosophically.

Porter raised his head. "Ward," he said, "if I can't go on would you mind if Tyne took over?"

Ward pulled out a dry blade of grass and placed it between his teeth. He stared out toward the road and turned the blade of grass moodily over in his mouth. "It don't make no difference to me," he said. "I don't care who's boss."

"Tyne's a good man," Porter said.

"I know he is," said Ward.

"You can work with him."

"I know I can."

"You can go on, Eddie," Tyne said.

"I don't know," said Porter. "I feel funny. I don't even know whether I'm sick or not. I just feel funny. Did you ever feel like you wanted to lie down and never get up?"

"Sure I have."

"That's the way I feel. Like I wanted to lie down and never get up."

"A guy gets tired after a while," said Ward. "You've been at it a long time."

"We've all been at it a long time," Porter said.

"Why don't you lie down a while, Eddie?" said Tyne. "You might feel better."

"I need a drink of water." Porter fumbled at his canteen and pulled it out of its cloth case. He pulled the canteen cup away from the bottom and unscrewed the top. That was one of Porter's idiosyncrasies: he never would drink from the mouth of the canteen, preferring always to use his cup. "Maybe I'd better lie down." He drank some water, screwed down the cap of the canteen, and laid cup and canteen beside him. Then he stretched out by the tree.

Ward ran some of the soil through his fingers. "Poor dirt," he said. "Poor country."

"Maybe if I rest," Porter said. He closed his eyes.

Archimbeau had watched the bubbles on his spittle for a long time. They fascinated him, reminding him of things insects made in the early morning at home. If you went out in the fields early you could see them. Spider spit, they were called. He didn't think spiders made them, but he supposed they could if they wanted to.

Suddenly Archimbeau pricked up his ears. There was the sound of a motor down the road, coming toward them. It didn't sound like a motorcycle, but that didn't mean that it couldn't be. These little hills could fool you. He raised himself on one knee and peered over the bush. In the direction of the farmhouse the road rose to a slight crest and then dipped. Beyond the dip, perhaps a hundred yards away, was another, slightly higher hill. He could see the crest of it. And as he looked out from behind the bush he saw, poking over the brow of the far hill, not a motorcycle, not a tank, but a lovely gleaming new armored car. It was German, and what it was doing moving over the road in their direction Archimbeau didn't wait to ask himself. He spun around, cupped his hands, and yelled "Armored car coming. Enemy armored car. Take cover!"

Then he fell flat behind his bush and took a grenade out of his pocket. Behind him the platoon scurried for cover.

# 8

SOMETIMES IT almost seems as though a man can throw up cover and concealment in his imagination and have it work. He can lie flat on the ground and will that he won't be seen, and he won't be. It is almost as though he could make himself invisible just by willing it. This is the last, most desperate cover of all, but it works a surprising number of times. If you have time you can fix things so that no one would ever be able to find you, but you've got to have the time. Even an hour can mean a lot. But it's when the planes come down or they come over the hill and surprise you that you start trying to push your face and stomach into the ground. When there's nothing over you it becomes necessary to will things. Otherwise you're a gone goose.

That was the way it was when the armored car came poking over the hill. The platoon heard Archimbeau yell, and then they all dived for the trees. There wasn't time to do anything else. They threw themselves behind the trunks and put their heads down and hung on. All of them, that is, except Porter. When he heard

Archimbeau's warning he merely rolled over on his stomach and burst into tears.

Tyne was behind a tree that was perhaps six inches thick and some three feet away from where he had been sitting. On one side of him Ward lay with his carbine beside him. He had his chin on the ground and was peering out toward the road. Tyne was conscious of Porter's body, lying completely in the open. Near the road he could see the soles of Archimbeau's feet where he lay behind his bush.

The armored car was a small one, used for light reconnaissance and carrying a crew of two, with one machine-gun poking out of a sawed-off turret behind the driver. Archimbeau watched it come toward him. The car was battened down completely, and the crew must have been pretty confident that there was no one around, because the turret was keeping still. If they'd been worried they'd have revolved it. The car was traveling slowly, taking its time. Archimbeau watched it as it came closer. He prepared to pull the pin from his grenade. Then, thinking better of it, he held off. The armored car came abreast of him and roared on down in the direction from which they had come. Archimbeau whistled lightly between his teeth. He looked up the road. Nothing. He scrambled around and crawled back on his belly to where the platoon was hiding behind its trees.

He saw Sergeant Porter lying on his stomach, facing away from the road. "Jesus Christ, Sarge," he said. "That was close."

"Leave him alone," Tyne said. "He's sick."

They spoke in whispers, as though the crew of the

armored car might hear them and come back. "What's the matter with him?" Archimbeau demanded.

"Sick," Tyne said. He came out from behind his tree and crouched down by Archimbeau. The platoon was beginning to show its heads again, peering out one and two at a time from behind the trunks and bushes that had served for concealment.

"Just that one?" Tyne asked.

"Guess so," Archimbeau said. "I almost threw a grenade at him."

"Good thing you didn't. What do you think, Ward?"

Sergeant Ward sat up behind his tree. "Damned if I know," he said. "I don't like it none."

"Go on back, Archimbeau," Tyne said. "Keep your eyes open."

"Why do I always have to pull this stuff?" Archimbeau demanded. "How about somebody else for a change?"

Tyne was taking grenades out of his pocket. "Okay," he said. "Get someone else."

"I'll do it," Riddle said. "Here, Arch, watch this god-damned gun. It gets in my way." He tossed his rifle to Archimbeau, who caught it in mid-air. Then he crawled back to the bush behind which Archimbeau had been hidden.

"I don't think there's more than one," Tyne said. "If they were sending a column along they wouldn't start it with a lousy armored car. It's just looking around to see how things are holding up down here. It'll be coming back this way pretty soon." He had completely forgotten Porter in the problem of the moment. Already he had reached the decision that the armored car would have to be got out of the way. He wasn't sure exactly how, though. Probably grenades would have to do.

"It'll be back all right," Ward said.

"I don't think we've got a hell of a lot of time. But we can probably knock it off with grenades if we're lucky. Those jobs don't weigh more than a couple of tons. A grenade under her belly ought to lift her right off the road. It'll shake up the driver, anyway."

Ward was toying with the bolt of his carbine. "How about machine-guns?" he asked.

"The tires," Tyne said. "We can get the tires. I don't know how much armor those babies carry. I've never seen one before."

"They didn't have anything like that in Africa," Archimbeau said.

"Old stuff," said Ward. "They got a lot of old stuff they're starting to use."

"It looked new."

"Paint."

Porter lay with his face in his hands. His bulky body heaved softly. Tyne shook his shoulder. "Eddie," he said. "Eddie."

"Leave me alone," Porter said. He jerked his shoulder under Tyne's hand. He was bad. It wasn't shock or anything like that. It was just a piling up of war. Porter had lived on his nerves for a long time, but he wasn't going to live off them any more. Porter was through, done. It had come quickly when it came. Yesterday he had been all right; now he was finished. It comes as fast as that when it does come. Porter had had his share of it; now he was for the cleaners.

126

"Leave him alone, Tyne," Ward said. "Nothing you can do."

"No," Tyne said. "What's the best way to work it? How about your squad? Set them down by the road, as close as they can get, and throw grenades on the whistle. Just on this side of the road, though. They'll be tossing grenades in each other's laps. Rivera!"

Rivera's black head, helmetless, poked up from behind a decaying stump. "What's up?"

"Come here, Rivera."

The addressed rose and came over in a crouching run. Behind him Friedman's eyes watched him go. Rivera flopped down beside Tyne. "Got a butt, Corporal?"

"No. How's your gun, doughfoot?"

"Okay."

"Set it up down there." Tyne's finger pointed to the fallen trunk of a tree a few yards from the road and about fifteen yards from where he was sitting, toward the east. "That car's coming back. We're going to try and get it with grenades. Now, when the grenades go off you let the car have it with all you've got. Rake it. *Compris?*"

"Yeah. Sure."

"Get it up in a hurry. Damn little time."

"Right." Rivera went back to his stump.

"Better line up your squad, Ward," Tyne said.

Ward got to his feet. "Okay, my squad," he said. "Off and on." Here and there a man rose to his feet and came over to join his sergeant.

"I got a job," Rivera said. "They just hired me. A hundred bucks a minute."

"It ain't enough," Friedman said.

"You coming?" Rivera asked.

"You mean I'm invited?"

"I got a silver-plated bullet with your name on it. Your name's Appleglotz, ain't it?"

"Yeah," Friedman said. "That's me, all right."

"Then you're invited."

"Then I'll come."

"That's good. Especially seeing as you've got the ammo."

"Now, you'll get a whistle," Ward said. "And so help me, the first bastard that throws before he gets the whistle will get a grenade right between his teeth. And for God's sake, throw straight. You won't get another chance. Johnson, you understand?"

"Yes, Sergeant."

"All right, then. You here. Randolph, you here." Quietly Ward went about placing his men. One at a time the whole squad stretched out flat. Each man had a grenade in his right hand and another one lying beside him. Tyne watched Ward place his men. So far the operation looked good. "Archimbeau," he said. "Watch Porter. Don't let him run around." He went over and joined Sergeant Ward. "Listen," he said to the rest of the platoon, "don't anyone else throw anything. Nobody at all, understand. We'll have enough men throwing things as it is. Just stay back where you are and hang on. You'll find out what happens soon enough." He turned to Ward. "Anyway, we know what happened to that rider."

"Sure do," Ward said.

"The only thing is, did they get him before he got

to the farmhouse or after he'd crossed the bridge?"

"For all we know he never crossed the bridge."

"Well, if they've got armor at the farmhouse we might just as well call the war off. I've got to pick myself a tree."

"Remember," Ward warned his squad. "On the whistle."

The platoon settled down to wait. Dimly between the trees the throb of artillery came to their ears, but they ignored it. They tried to hear over it, tried to catch the sound of a motor near at hand, the sound of the armored car returning up the road. The car couldn't have gone too far down; as it was it was more or less protected by the trees, but if it came out in the open country, by the ditch, one of the planes would be certain to see it. The crew of the armored car probably knew that; they'd go down as far as they figured it was safe to go and then they'd turn around and come back. They were just looking around, that was all, fronting for a far more powerful force farther inland.

It was a problem, the armored car. Tyne ran over in his mind the pros and cons of smashing it. Now that he had made all the decisions he wasn't sure that the decision to stop it was the right one. If the car didn't come back, whoever was up the road would think it funny; they might even send out a more powerful force to see what had happened to it. They could probably be sure that it wasn't the planes, because if the planes had come down on the road the Germans would have seen them; they'd have known what had stopped their shiny new armored car. But if the car

1 2 9

didn't come back and there was no reason for its not coming back—no reason that the Germans could see, that is—they might choose to conduct a little investigation, with three or four tanks, say, and then it would be good-by platoon. On the other hand, if they let the armored car go back it might report everything clear, and then the heavy armor might come along anyway. It was a ticklish thing for a man to make up his mind about. Tyne decided the best thing to do would be to get the car, because while the Germans were wondering what had happened to it the platoon might be able to get where it had to go. If the German armor was still on the other side of the river they had a good chance of success; if, however, the enemy was on the seaward side, it didn't much matter one way or the other. Once they knocked off the armored car they'd have to make time—good time. And they'd have to go through the woods into the bargain. They couldn't take the chance of meeting more vehicles on the road. They couldn't take any more chances at all.

Sun streamed through the trees and touched the dull barrel of Rivera's gun. He had wheedled a stick of gum from Friedman, and he felt rather better about things in general. He sat with his legs around the gun, a brand-new belt running through it, waiting. Occasionally he would pivot the gun an inch or two either way. "Ever go to Coney Island?" he asked.

"All the time," Friedman said. "Some joint."

"You ever shoot those electric guns that shoot down the airplanes?"

"Sure. I'm a shark at that stuff."

"You want to know a secret, Friedman?"

"You ain't got any secrets. You're an open book. You ain't bright enough to have any secrets."

"This is a secret, Jakie."

"What the hell is it?"

"I never could hit those airplanes. I used to miss those airplanes all the time."

"Maybe I'd better go away," Friedman said. "Maybe you ain't safe to be with. How'd you get to be a machine-gunner?"

"I bribed a guy."

"I want a transfer."

"Friedman, it's too late. You're stuck with me."

"Where you going to get that car, Rivera?"

Rivera licked his thumb and touched it on the barrel of his gun. I'm going to get every god-damned tire she's got. I'm going to aim for the knees. Then I work north."

"You think this stuff will go through armor?"

"Never has yet. You can't tell, though. Did you get a good look at that jalopy?"

"Pretty good."

"It looked old to me. It looked like they been saving that car for the last quarter. The old college try."

"It's still armor."

"You know Biddy Sims?"

"Corporal in B Company?"

"Yeah."

"What about him?"

"He got one of those big bastards with one of these babies. Explosive bullets. He just kept pounding away at the front of it. You pound away long enough and you're sure as hell going to get a few through the slits."

"I didn't know Biddy did that."

"He's a quick boy."

"Where is he now, anyway?"

Rivera waved an expressive hand in the direction of the artillery fire. "Down there, I guess. Maybe we been listening to him all morning, for all we know."

"Maybe he's going to listen to us for awhile now."

"You said it, Jakie boy."

Archimbeau studied Sergeant Porter's back incuriously. He could not understand what had happened to Porter; it was something beyond his comprehension. Wounds were simple. If a man was wounded he might yell or groan or keep his mouth shut, and whatever he did you knew what was the matter with him. But it was different with Porter. As he watched his big, heaving back Archimbeau was afraid, more afraid than he had been during the whole campaign. There was something terrible about the way Porter was crying. If he had been wounded it would have been a different story, but there was nothing the matter with him. He didn't have a mark on his body. It was as though something evil had entered him and shaken him the way a child shakes a rag doll and then thrown him down. Archimbeau felt that he would rather have been given any dirty detail than the one he had. He did not like to be with Porter. He felt that he had to do something. For a long time he stared at the sergeant's back; then he went over and lay down behind the tree that Tyne had been behind when the armored car had first come along.

The tears trickled through Porter's grubby fingers and dripped into the dry earth. Porter did not know why he was crying; he was hardly aware that he was crying at all. He had lost all track of the platoon and the objective and the war. He was beyond all of it. He dug the fingers of one hand into the ground. He wanted something solid under him; he was tired of ideas and orders and the unknown. He was tired of guesswork and waiting and wondering if what was going to happen was what should happen. He had taken refuge in himself, and nothing would shake him out of that secret lair. Sergeant Porter had taken unto himself the final cover, the last concealment. He was unaware of the armored car; he was unaware that it was day, and that there were noises in the distance, and that he was human. All that came through his consciousness was that he was very tired and alone.

Over his shoulder Tyne looked at Porter. Nothing he could do. He fingered the whistle in his hand and then watched Riddle. Riddle had the best view of the road of any of them. He was peering anxiously down the dusty tracks; occasionally he would look back and shake his head. Nothing. Tyne's mind flashed ahead to the farmhouse. He tried to picture it. Must have a look at the map when this was done. There was no compass in his pocket; he had lost the one he had in Sicily and had never replaced it. Probably Ward would have one or, failing that, Porter. They'd have to go by compass through the woods. Tyne imagined that they had about a mile to go—certainly no farther. With luck they would be in the farmhouse within an hour.

The arms of Private Riddle suddenly tensed and he reared up on them, peering out beyond his bush. He's heard something, Tyne said to himself. He saw Ward staring at Riddle intently. Riddle turned toward Tyne and nodded his head in an affirmative. The armored car was coming back. "Easy," Ward said in a low voice. His squad clung to the ground, their faces set.

Riddle went flat again. He laid his face on the ground so that there was a mere narrow slit between the grass and the rim of his helmet. From twenty feet away he would have resembled a small, remarkably smooth stone. In the slit between grass and helmet he framed the armored car as it came into sight. It was still battened down, but the turret was motionless; evidently the suspicions of the crew were lulled. They had gone down to the edge of the open country, had observed, and had seen nothing. Now, on their way back, they were taking it easy. The car was moving at about twenty miles an hour, heaving as its wheels rose and sank in the ruts.

It came closer. Rivera, behind his log, bent over the machine-gun, lining the armored car up. He was humming under his breath—not a definite tune, but simply a low murmuration of three or four notes. He sighted along the barrel and picked up the right front tire of the armored car. He held his sights there.

It was necessary to give the car ten seconds' leeway. Tyne closed his eyes for a fraction of a second in silent prayer that everything would go well. The car was almost at the spot he had picked. It was traveling at

1 3 4

the speed he wanted it to travel. He counted slowly to himself. One. Two. Three. He brought the whistle swiftly up to his lips and blew it as hard as he could.

Tyne was conscious of many arms moving back and throwing their missiles. The noise of the car seemed to become deafening. He knew that he should put his head down, but he couldn't bring himself to do it. The armored car suddenly picked up speed. The driver had seen the grenades. Now it was directly abreast of him. He realized that, unknown to himself, he had been counting aloud. "Nine," he said. As he said it two of the grenades went off, one a few feet behind the car and another directly under it. The car rose like a bucking horse and fell back heavily. The nose pointed toward the side of the road. And even as it hit, the road exploded in a sheet of flame as the other grenades went off. Rivera's machine-gun began its chatter. The car disappeared in smoke. Tyne felt something smash against the side of his helmet—probably a stone or a bit of steel. He tried to peer through the smoke. It was clearing, very slowly. Bits of rock began falling around him.

"God damn it," Rivera shouted. "God-damned smoke. Any time you get a bead on something the god-damned smoke comes along." He was firing blindly. Friedman tapped him on the shoulder. "The corporal says to hold it," he shouted in his ear. Rivera looked toward Tyne. The corporal was standing up, waving at him. He released his finger from the trigger.

The smoke had cleared around the armored car. It was lying on its side. One wheel was spinning idly. The belly, facing them, was bent inward. There were no holes in it that they could see. "Rankin," Tyne said. "Put a few shots through one of the slits."

Rankin hopped to his feet, his tommy-gun at the alert, and trotted out to the armored car. He put the gun in the driver's eye slit and pulled the trigger. Lead smashed against the car's interior as he moved the muzzle up and down. He put about thirty shots into the car. Probably the two men who made up the crew had been alive when he started shooting; if so, they were not alive now. The platoon had no time to take prisoners.

Tyne walked out to the car, Sergeant Ward at his heels. Two members of Ward's squad started to follow them. "Stay where you are," Tyne said. "There's nothing out here you haven't seen before."

He bent down and peered through the driver's slit. It was full of smoke inside; all around there was the bitter, acrid smell of burned powder. Dimly he could discern two crumpled figures. He suddenly realized that a hand was hanging limply very near his eye. There was a huge ring on the index finger. "Funny place to have a ring," he thought. It was a red stone, perhaps a ruby.

Straightening, Tyne looked up the road in the direction of the farmhouse. "I don't know whether they heard all the noise," he said, "but whether they did or not we'd better get the hell out of here. There's more where this came from." He kicked the car gently; it gave off a hollow sound. "You got a compass, Ward?"

"Think so," Ward said. He reached in his left pocket. "Yep, here's one. Good one, too. Never had a bit of trouble with that compass." He gave it to Tyne. Together they walked back into the woods.

"Get that gun down, doughfoot," Tyne said as he passed Rivera.

"Some smoke screen," Rivera said. "Like a christly battleship."

"That car's probably full of holes," Friedman said.

"Like a cheese," Rivera said. "Like a god-damned cheese."

"I'll bet you never put a hole in it."

"I never miss."

"How about the airplanes at Coney Island?"

"That was Coney Island. Those were airplanes."

"Okay, Rivera, you're a terror."

"I sure as hell am."

"I've got to take a look at the map," Tyne said. "Got to get some sort of beam on the house."

"Porter's got it," Ward said.

"I know."

He bent down and opened the map case, which was lying at Porter's side. From it he pulled the map of the surrounding country, opened it, and spread it on the ground. It seemed that this was the fiftieth time that morning he had spread out the map. By rights it should have been frayed and torn, with all the handling it had received. But it was new and neat and glossy. The only mark on it was a fingerprint in blood. That had probably come from Hoskins.

"I'm a killer, all right," Rivera said. "I don't know what this platoon would do without me."

"Win the god-damned war," Friedman said.

"That's right," said Rivera. "Win the god-damned war."

# 9

I T's WOODS all the way," Tyne said, "if we're where I think we are."

"It looks right," Ward said. He wiggled his finger along the map. "The road twisted like hell in here."

"All level till we hit this field in front of the farm," Tyne said. "What's the course?"

"West-south-west, I guess," said Ward. "I'd hold it right on there. Just about a mile to go."

Tyne measured with his index finger. "Just about. Take us a half hour if we move fast and hit it right."

The river cut around the farm and came toward them, about a quarter of a mile from where they were. If they got too far off in that direction the river would put them right; on the other side was the road. They could hardly miss it. "How do we line up now?" Tyne said. He surveyed the platoon. "Craven."

Craven, a sad-faced man, came over, swinging his helmet in his hand. He was nearly bald. "Take over my squad, will you, Craven?"

"Sure, Bill."

"Johnson, you stay here with the sergeant. Can you spare him, Ward? Okay. Stay here with the sergeant.

Don't let him do anything. Just keep him here. Understand?"

"What if he tries to go somewhere?"

"Don't let him."

"How?"

"I don't care how. Don't let him, that's all. Wait a minute." Tyne bent down by Porter and shook him gently. "How are you feeling, Eddie?"

Sergeant Porter's nails dug into the ground. There was no other answer.

"Okay, Johnson," Tyne said. "Watch him. Arch, you and Cousins get going. If you see anything, just shoot. Let's go."

The scouts moved out into the woods. "You got the direction, Arch?" Tyne called after them.

"Can't miss," Archimbeau called back. Tyne fell into his place at the head of the column. To the sound of feet on leaves they moved through the woods, past Porter, past Johnson, toward the exploding war.

They all felt better somehow. The fact that they had knocked out the armored car had cheered them considerably. It no longer mattered that they weren't exactly sure where they were going or what they would find there. They had seen their own powers redisplayed. The morning had been bad, entirely bad, until they had run up against the car. Now the balance had shifted. They were no longer oppressed by what awaited them up ahead. They felt that they could handle it, together or singly. They had their morale back.

Not that they had ever really lost it. They had simply been a little uncertain of themselves. They were out of practice. But all in all they were a good platoon, a very good platoon. They worked well together; for the most part they understood each other. That was an essential. In its way war is like a lethal game of football. The squad is a team, the platoon is a team, the company is a team. So are the regiment and the army. It is no longer enough to kill two of them before they kill you: the thing is to kill two of them and stay alive.

Moving between the trees, Archimbeau felt that he had had a bad morning. First there was Trasker and then the sergeant. He had almost forgotten Trasker now. What had happened to him had been a natural thing. It might have happened to anybody. But the sergeant haunted him. Any wound that was not caused by some external object terrified Archimbeau. "I am not afraid of drunks," his mother once said, "but I'm afraid of crazy people." So was Archimbeau, the dutiful son, the lonely bachelor. Dimly he wondered if Porter had gone crazy. He knew it wasn't shell-shock, because he had seen guys get shell-shocked, and when that happened it was because a shell had hit near them. Simple, like everything else in the Army. Simple, like the road to Tibet. But no shell had hit near Sergeant Porter. He had just gone off for no reason. Still, Archimbeau always thought that crazy people ran around with knives. Maybe the sergeant wasn't crazy after all. Maybe he was just sick.

He was not keeping a very careful watch. For one thing, there wasn't much you could hide behind the trees, and there were no bushes to speak of. For another, he had decided that there was nothing on this

140

side of the river. He didn't know why he had reached this decision; he just felt that it was true. Archimbeau was a great man for intuition.

"Did you ever go camping when you was a kid?" Rivera asked.

"Every time we get in a bunch of trees you ask me that same question," Friedman said.

"Every time I get in a bunch of trees I remember it," said Rivera.

"For the millionth time, no, I never went camping when I was a kid. I lived in the city."

"I lived in the city, too, for Christ's sake. I got on a train."

"You told me."

"Well, I'm telling you again."

"You're a juke box, Rivera. Somebody keeps putting nickels in you."

"I ain't talking to you any more. Hey, Judson, you ever go camping in the woods?"

"What woods?"

"Get that, will you? Any woods."

"Naw."

"Judson, you don't know what you missed. You ain't ever lived until you toasted a mickey over the coals. It ain't like the Army crap. You can sit around a campfire, see, and shoot it all night if you want to. You can go fishing. All that kind of stuff."

"Outdoor man," Friedman said.

"Next time they make you a civilian, Judson," Rivera said, "try a camp in the woods. Just tell them I sent you."

"Tell who?"

"The birds and the bees. Didn't your old man ever tell you about the birds and the bees?"

"Naw."

"You hear that, Friedman? Judson never heard of the birds and the bees."

Friedman was on firm ground now. "Terrible," he said.

"Shall we tell him?"

"Maybe we better."

Rivera held out his hand. "Give us a butt, Judson, and we'll tell you all about the birds and the bees."

"I ain't got a butt," Judson said sadly.

In his mind Craven was trying to frame a letter to his sister. He figured that if he could think it out now he could write it later from memory and save time. "Dear Frances," he began. "This is the first letter I have written you from Italy. I am now sitting down in an old farmhouse. We have just blown up a bridge near here . . ." No, that wouldn't do. Best to keep it indefinite. "Dear Frances, I am writing this from somewhere in Italy but I don't exactly know where because we have been moving so fast that I haven't had time to read the signs." No, cross that out. "—Because we haven't seen any signs. For all I know it isn't even Italy but it will do until the next country comes along. It is a bright, sunny day, very warm, so maybe I am in Sunny Italy after all (ha, ha) and if I am I'll send you a barrel of Chianti." No, "Cianti." Neither way seemed right. That was the hell of foreign words. Italian was as bad as French.

He turned to Private Tinker, who was walking beside him. "Tinker," he said, "how do you spell 'Chianti'?"

"What's that?"

"It's a wine. A wop wine."

"Never heard of it."

"What's the matter with you? Don't you drink?"

"Sure I drink," Tinker said. "You've seen me drink. I never heard of the stuff, that's all."

"It's a red wine. You drink it with dinner and stuff."

"The hell with this wine junk. When I drink I want to feel I been drinking something. Applejack. Rye. That's the stuff."

"Don't you think I know it, for God's sake?" Craven said. "I was drinking that stuff when they were feeding you milk. I just wanted to know how to spell it, that's all."

"Why?"

"I'm writing to my sister."

Tinker stared at him. "What do you mean, you're writing to your sister? You're walking through some god-damned woods, that's what you're doing."

"I'm writing the letter in my head, see? Then when I get a minute I just put down what I remember in my head, and the letter's all written. It's the best way."

"Jesus," Tinker said, "what a system. Does it work?"

"Sure," said Craven.

"You just make up the letter in your head while you're walking and then write it down later?"

"Yeah."

"Hey, that's pretty good. Maybe I'll try it. It works, huh?"

"Every time." •

"Suppose you got a bad memory?"

"You got a bad memory?"

"I got a good one."

"Then why you worrying?"

"I'm not. I just wondered. What was that word you wanted to spell?"

"Chianti."

Tinker wrinkled his brow. "Never heard of it," he said. "They don't have it in St. Paul."

The easiest thing would be to forget it, Craven decided. The easiest thing would be to begin again. "Dear Frances, I am writing this letter from Somewhere in Italy, but I don't know where because they haven't told me yet. I am well and hope you are the same. Did you get a letter from Frank?"

There were little bare patches in the wood, as though someone had chopped down a dozen trees and dug out the stumps. Once they passed the foundation of a house, covered with dry grass. Time had played with it, and the forest had taken over. It was impossible to tell how old the house was. Tyne studied it carefully as he went past. Italy, he knew, was full of ruins. Rome had the most of all. Perhaps the foundation was that of a Roman house, and perhaps they were the first who had seen it in two thousand years. But people had been in the woods since then. Here and there a stump stuck from the ground, and once he saw a faded piece of paper. Tyne remembered the ruins of Tunisia, standing by themselves miles from any human habitation. Little Arab boys had sold them Roman coins. Statues had been found around the broken temples, and once a doughfoot, digging a slit trench, had broken through into a Roman grave, the grave of a woman. Time had left of her a pot of money and a few hairpins. It was enough; it was a memorial.

He looked at his watch. They had been on the move nearly a quarter of an hour; nearly halfway on the last lap. When he thought of the farm he felt his spine tingle, as though somewhere in his body there was a buzzer that was a warning.

He had always had that feeling when something was about to happen. First the buzzer would go and then he would feel weak. He wiped the sweat from his forehead; it had run down into his eyebrows and from there was finding its way into his eyes. A tingle and a weak feeling. It was not necessarily a warning of danger. It was, on the contrary, the body preparing itself, releasing reserves of energy and strength—nothing more than that. Tyne certainly did not feel afraid. He felt rather giddy and lightheaded and confident. The giddiness was part of the weak feeling. It would pass. But the confidence would stay with him. Only when the platoon had done what it had been sent to do would the confidence leave him. Then he would sink into a melancholy. It was a reaction, and it had happened to him before. He was powerless to stop it. But while he had the confidence he would put it to good use.

Archimbeau, he noticed, was getting too far ahead. He seemed in a hell of a hurry to get somewhere.

Private James and Carraway were talking about Life.

145

"If you aren't on the ball, you haven't got a chance," Private James said. "You got to be smart these days."

"I don't know," said Private Carraway. "Look at the freaks in the circus."

"Aw, they don't count. They're freaks."

"They ain't smart, but they pull in the dough."

"I mean the average guy."

"The average guy ain't smart, for Christ's sake."

"That ain't what I'm trying to say," Private James said. "I mean that the competition is tough. If you don't keep on the ball some bright boy is going to slip in and nab your job. That's life. That's what I was trying to say."

"If you're good nobody's going to take your job."

"That's what I mean. You got to be good."

"You can be good and still be a dope," said Carraway.

"How do you get that?"

"All right, suppose you can run a machine better than anyone else. Do you have to have brains to run the machine? Naw, you don't need any brains. It's a purely mechanical process. Anybody could learn to do it."

"All right, let's get back to where I was in the first place, then. The competition is tough."

"All right, it's tough."

"Life ain't no joke these days."

"All right, it ain't a joke. Was it ever a joke?"

"How do I know? I haven't lived all the time."

"How do you think a guy would like it, living all the time?"

"I wouldn't like it," James said. "You'd get in a rut."

"How do you mean?"

"History's all the same. Life's all the same. You'd be doing the same thing all the time, over and over again."

"I'd like to try it, just the same," Carraway said.

"There'd still be the competition."

The sun was soaring toward the highest reaches of heaven. It blazed down malevolently. Their helmets became like ovens; their clothes stuck to their bodies. They were bathed from head to foot in their own perspiration. When a man is uncomfortable, through either heat or cold, he finds it hard to think consecutively. His thoughts come in flashes. He is too conscious of his ever-present discomfort. The body, as always, thwarts the mind. The minutes develop a talent for moving slowly, for crawling around the face of the clock. Everything seems to stand still. The whole world simmers in a gigantic pot. The air actually has weight and body, and it seems to stagnate, like still water. Smells have a dull, unpleasant pungency. It is difficult to think of food. Anything with an odor repels one.

Yet Sergeant Ward still thought of apples. They were becoming a mirage, dancing in front of his eyes, dripping with juice. He would gladly have given three months' pay for a cold apple, a big red juicy one. There was nothing cold he could have. The water in his canteen was tepid, and so was all the ration he carried. The thought of apples taunted him, and to get it off his mind he thought of other images—of a cold well and of cold well water, of cider cold and fresh from the jug, of ice cream. The new images did not help him. If anything they made things worse, and when he cast them out of his mind the idea of apples still flaunted itself and would not be shaken out.

"Like to have an apple," he said to Riddle.

"Yeah," Riddle said. "What I wouldn't give for a beer. A nice cold glass of beer. Just one."

"I been thinking of apples all day," Ward said.

"Apples and oranges," said Riddle.

"Funny thing is, I don't like apples."

"A guy always wants something when he can't get it."

"Yeah."

The funny thing was that they were not very much concerned with what was facing them ahead. Each had his own problems, his own desires and wishes. They kept these personal things uppermost in their minds, as they had always done ever since they came into the Army. The war was incidental to a man's thoughts. It entered into them, of course, but it did not take them over bodily. There had been too many years of life, too many memories, before the war had come along. A man could exist on these memories, he could withdraw into them, he could construct them into an unpierceable shell. They were his defence against the violence of the world. Every man in the platoon had his own thoughts as he walked along, and they hovered unseen over the little group, an indefinable armor, a protection against fate, an indestructible essence.

"It's a good thing they invented trains for traveling salesmen," Rivera said.

"All right," Friedman said. "Kill me. What's the gag?"

"No gag," said Rivera. "But if they didn't have trains all the traveling salesmen would have to walk. A hell of a job that would be."

"You're a traveling salesman," Friedman said. "And you ain't been taking any trains lately."

"What do you mean, I'm a traveling salesman? I'm a murderer."

"You're a traveling salesman. You're selling democracy to the natives."

Rivera was silent for a moment. "So that's what I am, huh? Well, what do you know. Where'd you get that crap, Jakie?"

"Out of a book."

"A book."

"You're a decadent democrat, Rivera."

"That's what I am, all right. But to get back to traveling salesmen, how many of those Joes do you think would of become traveling salesmen if they'd had to walk everywheres?"

"I don't know," Friedman said. "I never knew a traveling salesman."

"Maybe I'll be one after the war," Rivera said. "You get to cover a hell of a lot of territory."

"Baby," said Friedman, "you've covered a hell of a lot of territory, and you ain't nothing."

"Friedman," Rivera said, "I been good to you. Every time you needed it I always gave you my last franc. I treated you like a brother. And every time you get the chance you needle me up the back. What kind of stuff is that?"

"I'm anti-social," Friedman said. "I got gap-osis."

"Maybe you should go off somewhere."

"Where?"

"How should I know? I treat you like a brother and you stick a knife in my back. He's a crumb, ain't he, Judson?"

"Everybody's a crumb," Judson said. "I wish I was home in bed."

"Anybody who would sleep in the noontime is a dope," said Rivera.

"He's a dope," Friedman said.

If the bridge was steel, Tyne thought, they'd really have a job on their hands. They'd have one if it was concrete, too. If it was wood, though, it shouldn't be too much trouble. He ran over the possibilities in his mind. There was a chance that the bridge might already have been bombed and the Jerries only had a makeshift job crossing the river. That was a very good possibility. The planes had been bombing around this area for a couple of weeks. If they had knocked out the bridge and it had been repaired they could be sure it would be a wooden affair.

Suddenly it dawned on Tyne that there had actually been no orders given to blow up a bridge at all. It had been decided within the platoon that the bridge had to be blown. It was very strange. Certainly if they had wanted to blow the bridge they would have sent the planes or, failing that, a bunch of demolition boys from the Engineers. It was damned queer. Tyne felt that he had to run over the entire situation again.

There was a farmhouse. That was certain. What was uncertain was whether or not the farmhouse was occupied by the enemy. That was point one. And there was a bridge. That was certain. What was uncertain was whether the bridge had already been blown or not. That was point two. And there were several courses of action. If the farmhouse was unoccupied and the bridge hadn't been blown, they would have to blow the bridge and occupy the farmhouse. If the farmhouse was unoccupied and the bridge was blown, they'd merely have to occupy the farmhouse and see that no one built up the bridge again. If the farmhouse was occupied and the bridge was blown, they'd have to take the farmhouse and watch the bridge. That might not be easy. And if the farmhouse was occupied and the bridge was unblown, they'd have a good-sized chunk of hell, sitting up warm and wicked, right in their hands. Four possibilities. Tyne tried to reason out the one that was probably right. He wanted to wish that the bridge was smashed to bits and the farmhouse was empty, but that didn't hold water. The armored car had either come from the farmhouse or over the bridge, so it was safe to say that something ran across the water. The armored car would have had to get to the farm in the first place. And in that event the farm was occupied and the river was bridged. The more Tyne ran the picture through his mind the darker it became. At last he had reached the conclusion that the farmhouse might very well be occupied, and that there was some sort of bridge over the river. The Germans were never men to pass over river crossings.

He suddenly whirled and strode back to where Ward

was bringing up his squad. "I've been thinking it over," he said. "I think we're going to run into trouble."

"I thought that all along," Ward said quietly. "Jerry's smart. He isn't missing a trick."

"I think they've got someone in that farmhouse," Tyne said.

Ward spat solemnly. "That's what I think," he said. "They probably got a machine-gun in every goddamned window in the place."

"They've got something across the river, too," Tyne said. "I don't think it's a regular bridge, but they've got something."

"Yeah," said Sergeant Ward. He was a man of opinion.

Tyne went back to his place at the head of the column. Archimbeau was getting even farther ahead. Tyne broke into a run, caught up with him, and caught him by the arm. "Take it easy, Arch," he said. "Don't get too far ahead."

"Didn't know I was," Archimbeau said. "I was almost asleep on my feet. I didn't get any sleep at all last night."

"Well, keep awake now."

"Okay. Say, Corp, do you think I'll make Pfc. by the Battle of Tibet?"

"Sure. They'll make you a general."

"That's all I wanted to know. How much farther's this farm?"

Tyne looked at his watch. "We ought to be breaking into the field below it any time now. Keep your eyes open, for God's sake, and stop when you see the field."

"Right."

On his way back to his place Tyne winked at Rankin. "How's it going, Tim?"

"I been here before," Rankin said.

By mutual consent, without any command being spoken, the men talked in whispers. They knew that they were approaching their objective. They walked more lightly and they began to look around them, peering through the trees as though they expected to see someone. The woods had suddenly become dangerous. No one could say at what point they had taken on a menacing aspect, but it had happened in a twinkling. Perhaps it had been when Tyne had run up toward the scouts. Any unforeseen movement could put a man on his guard or on the alert. Tenseness came over them, and their legs felt stiff. They almost seemed to walk stiff-legged, like angry dogs. The war had finally caught up with them.

Rankin looked at his tommy-gun. It was beautifully oiled and in perfect condition. Rankin took good care of his gun; he treated it as though it were a highly sensitive infant. He slept with it cradled beside him. There was only one thing about it that made it stand out, however. Scratched on its barrel were eleven lines. The eleven lines stood for soldiers of the Third Reich—for ex-supermen—moldering into dust in Tunisia and Sicily. They were Rankin's certains; he never counted the probables.

"Some day," Rivera said, "I'm going to walk into a country and they're going to put out a rug that says 'Welcome' and they're going to let me walk in on it. That's what I'm going to do some day."

"When?" Friedman asked.

"Next Tuesday, for Christ's sake. How the hell do I know when? In 1983."

"I'll look you up then."

"This is a hell of a way to see Europe."

"Ah, if it hadn't been for this war the nearest you'd ever of got to Europe would be the Staten Island ferry."

"Anybody can go to Europe. I know a guy worked his way over on a cattle boat."

"Why?"

"He wanted to see it."

"He must have been a hell of a dope."

"He was my cousin."

"Then I know he was a hell of a dope."

"After we get up to this farmhouse I'm going to take you out in the dung shed and beat the bejesus out of you."

"What with?"

"The barrel of this god-damned gun."

"Okay. I thought you were going to really get tough."

"That farmhouse is sure as hell full of Krauts."

"It sure as hell is."

"Friedman, I'm glad I brought this gun along. I'm glad they gave it to me."

"Between you and me, old boy, I am too."

"A butt."

Friedman sighed. "I can remember the days when I had one," he said.

Archimbeau's arm went straight up in the air and he stopped in his tracks. Every man in the column fell suddenly silent. Tyne walked ahead. "Coming out of the woods," Archimbeau said. He pointed. In the direction of his finger, perhaps fifty yards away, Tyne could see light through the trees and a gentle brown slope. "That's it, all right," he said.

Ward came along. "On the nose," he said.

"On the nose."

"What do you think?"

"I don't know yet. I'm going up and take a look. Arch, you come along."

"Take it easy," Ward said.

Silently Tyne and Archimbeau moved through the trees. Tyne carried his rifle loosely in his right hand; Archimbeau had his on the sling. As they moved away from the platoon the wood seemed to open up like a flower. Light streamed in on them, reflected from the field. They walked slower and slower. Once Tyne thought he caught the glint of something far up in the field—it could have been a helmet—and he stopped in his tracks. It was almost as though he was sniffing the air. Then he moved on, more cautiously. Archimbeau followed closely at his heels.

When they were almost at the edge of the wood Tyne could see an old wall, made of some kind of stone and mortar, running along the fringe of trees. He fell on his belly and wiggled the last few yards to the wall, Archimbeau crawling behind him. And then, when they were both safely behind the wall, Tyne cautiously raised his head and peered out on the field —a brown world, full of high brown grass and the sighings of late insects.

# 10

THE FIELD was a hill that stretched a hundred and
fifty yards up to a farmhouse with a red tile roof.
Here and there a boulder marred its surface, and
there were patches where the grass lay flat. It looked
as though it had been trampled. Tyne counted four
out-buildings; it was quite a large farm. The house
had been painted or whitewashed quite recently. He
could see no movement around the buildings. "I wish
to God I had those binoculars now," he said.

"Can you see anything?"

"Not a damned thing."

"How about the windows?"

"Sun's on them."

To the right the wood curved around, along what
evidently was the bank of the river. The wall seemed
to stop down there. "I wish I knew," Tyne said. "I
wish to God I knew."

"Knew what?" Archimbeau asked.

"Nothing. Let's go back."

They moved back on their stomachs. After a while
Tyne stood up. Archimbeau also rose, and they broke

into a fast walk. The platoon was waiting for them. Half the men were sitting or lying down; the rest were leaning against trees or just standing around. "How's it look?" Ward said.

"Quiet. But I don't like it. Too quiet."

Ward nodded. "They're bad when they're too quiet."

"Craven," Tyne said. He fell on his knees and picked up a stick. Craven came over to where he was kneeling, and Tyne drew a rough line along the ground. "There's a stone wall that runs along here for about two or three hundred yards, probably between the road and the river. There's a clear slope up to the farmhouse from the wall. Not much cover. The wall seems to stop where the river curves around the farm, but there are trees running along the river bank. There doesn't seem to be any movement among the farm buildings. It's hard to tell just what the story is. If I had a pair of binoculars I'd have been able to see more."

"Think there's anyone there?" Craven asked.

"That's what I don't know," said Tyne. "Anyway, we aren't going to take any chances. We'll send a patrol up first, four or five guys."

"I'll take it," Ward said suddenly.

"I may need you here," Tyne said.

"I want to take it," Ward said.

Tyne studied his face. "Okay," he said. "You take it. Pick yourself four men."

"I'll go," Rivera said.

"No, you won't, doughfoot," Tyne said. "I need your little instrument."

"I want four volunteers," Ward said. "Four Congressional-Medal-of-Honor-with-ten-oak-leaf-clusters volunteers."

"Any extra pay?" Rankin wanted to know.

"Naw."

"Then I'll go anyway," Rankin said. "Just to make them feel ashamed."

"I'm a hero," Cousins said. "I been up front all day. I might as well stay there."

"I'll go along," Tranella said.

"The first guys that get to that house will get the wine," Tinker said. "I'll go."

"Okay," Ward said. "That's four."

"Pass out the Purple Hearts, mother," Rivera said.

"All right," Tyne said. "We'll go up to the wall in column, then fan out when we get there. The wall's three feet high. There's plenty of room. But don't let me catch any son of a bitch sticking his head up in the air. When you fan out keep about five yards apart. Craven, you take your squad down toward the road. Riddle, you take Ward's squad down toward the river. My squad will stay in the center. Rivera, you take your popgun down by the road, so you can keep your eye on the farmhouse and the road at the same time. Got that, doughfoot?"

"It's in my head," Rivera said.

"Keep it there. And remember to cover if anyone needs it."

"Okay, chief."

"Let's go." Tyne moved through the woods. The platoon straggled after him, moving as silently as Indians. As Tyne came nearer to the field he was struck with the same feeling of the wood's unfolding like a flower that he had had the first time. He hit the dirt at almost the same place as before. One by one the men flopped down after him.

He stopped at the wall and directed traffic, to right and left. The men wiggled along the wall or moved at a crouch, careful not to hunch their backs too high. Ward and his volunteers hugged the wall near Tyne. "Might as well go over right here," Ward said.

Tyne considered a minute. "I guess so," he said. "Maybe we're getting worried for nothing. Maybe there's no one up there after all."

"I think there is," Ward said.

"What are you going to do?"

"Well," Ward said, "if we can get within grenade-throwing distance we'll be all right. Let me take a look and see." He raised his head a little over the wall and studied the terrain. When he pulled his head down again he was frowing. "Don't look too good at that," he said. "A few boulders, but not a hell of a lot else. That grass won't do much good."

"It'll help," Tyne said.

"Yeah, it'll help."

Most of the men were in position. "We'll wait till Rivera gets his gun up," Tyne said. "Give him five minutes. If anything goes wrong he'll cover you."

"If anything goes wrong, shoot for the windows," Ward said. "That's where they'll be. They like the windows."

"I know."

Warily Tyne took another look over the wall. Things did not seem to have changed. Nothing had moved around the farmhouse. The windows still reflected the sun. Certainly there was nothing about the farm to arouse suspicion. But that was the way it always was. The things to watch out for were the things that looked innocent. That was the principle of booby traps.

"Why are you so anxious to take a patrol?" Tyne asked.

"I don't know," Ward said. "I just am."

Down at the far end of the woods, by the road, Rivera and Friedman were finishing setting up the gun. "You can hit anything from here," Friedman said. "They ought to have portable walls to go with every war."

"I'll see they have them next time," Rivera said. "I wouldn't want you to be disappointed."

"This is a pretty good spot."

"It'll do for awhile. I ain't planning to raise a family here."

"How's the farm look?"

"I'll rake that joint."

"I think it's okay," Tyne said. "Got enough grenades?"

"Yeah," Ward said. He studied the four men who were to go with him. "We'll stay five yards apart," he said. "And keep on your gut, for God's sake. Spread out, now."

The four men strung themselves along behind the wall. "Good luck," Tyne said.

"The same to you," Ward said. He looked to the right and left. "Over," he said. He leaped over the wall and lay flat in the grass. The other men followed him.

All up and down the line of the wall there was silence. Silence hung over the farmhouse, too. Far away could be heard the dull rumble of artillery, but it was cut off in great measure by the intervening woods. Ward hugged the ground, listening. He could see none of the other members of the patrol because of the high grass. Now he wished he had not had them stay five yards apart. A guy could wander away, especially if he was on the end. Stiffly Ward began to move forward.

The patrol had a long way to go. He moved fast. Near him he could hear the other men moving forward. Beneath the grass the ground was rough. It stuck to his sweat-soaked fatigues. He seemed to grate on the earth as he crawled along. A boulder reared before him, and he skirted it. As he did so he caught sight of Tinker in a bare patch. He winked at him. Tinker licked his lips with his tongue and made a half-wave.

Tyne slowly raised his head over the wall. The patrol was moving steadily up the slope. He could see two figures; the other three he could locate only by the waving of the grass. One of the figures was in a bare patch, the other was behind a boulder. They had gone perhaps fifty yards.

Suddenly, as though by instinct, he knew that something was going to happen. It was like those times when people see a man who is actually dying a thousand miles away. One moment everything was all right, and the next Tyne wanted to yell out for the patrol to come back.

He saw smoke drift from one of the windows of the house, and the next minute the noise of a machine-gun came to his ears. The Germans had opened up. The farm was occupied, all right, very well occupied. Tyne jerked his head down, looked at the man nearest him, and shook his head. "God damn," he said over and over again. "God damn. God damn. God damn."

The machine-gun had started up so suddenly that it had taken Ward by surprise. Off to his left he could hear bullets hitting the ground and singing away. It was too hot a place, much too hot. "Go back," he yelled. "Patrol back." He turned around and began to crawl down the slope. He could see the wall beckoning to him. It was hard to believe that anything so near could be so far away. He passed the boulder again and saw Tinker again, crawling back with him. This time he did not wink. He hugged the ground as a line of bullets parted the air over his head.

Slowly Tyne peered over the wall again. Why the hell didn't they come back? But they were coming. Good. He could see the grass waving as they worked their way toward the wall, and he could see the grass swaying as the machine-gun traversed it. "Tell Rivera to let her go," he said to the man on his left. The word went down the line.

Ward was wondering why Rivera didn't open up. He was cut off from the rest of the patrol, and he didn't know whether or not any of them had been hit. He was conscious only of his own efforts and the wall luring him on. His mouth was very dry, and he regretted coming out with the patrol. There had been just a chance that the farm had been unoccupied. He had known the chance was slim—he hadn't believed it himself, but he had wanted to take it. He dug dirt again as a row of bullets passed over him.

"Jesus Christ, here goes," Rivera said. The gun jumped and shivered before him. Far away, along the wall of the house, Friedman could see dust rise as the slugs cut into the mortar. "Get that bloody window," he said. Rivera obligingly lowered the muzzle of the gun an almost imperceptible distance. Bullets smashed through the window and into the house. The German machine-gun went suddenly silent.

"Let me be the first to congratulate you," Friedman said solemnly. He held out his hand.

Ward heard Rivera's gun go into action. It was home and music to him. He stopped and listened. He was almost certain he could hear Rivera's slugs smash into the side of the house. Behind him the German machine-gun went dead. He raised his head and took a quick look over his shoulder. Dust and mortar were flying from the house and glass spattered from the windows as Rivera raked it back and forth. Ward grinned mirthlessly. Rivera kept his finger on the trigger. Might as well make a run for it, Ward said to himself.

He calculated the distance to the wall. It was perhaps twenty yards, an easy run. Ward did not bother to think the situation out in any detail. There wasn't time. He suddenly stood upright in the field. "Cousins, Rankin," he shouted. "Everybody over the wall." Three figures rose up from the grass. They all bolted for the long wall. Rivera's gun chattered on. Five yards from the wall Sergeant Ward heard rifle fire from the house. He leaped to the right and zigzagged back again. He went over the wall head first, in a giddy dive. Cousins and Tranella leaped after him. Tinker was slow, at least two yards behind the others. He wasn't zigzagging. As he reached the wall there were three scattered shots from the house. Tinker tossed his rifle in the air and fell forward against the wall, his body half crawling up the rough stone. His hand hung over the top. Far away, on the left, Rivera's gun stopped firing.

Ward lay flat for a moment. His leap had nearly knocked the wind out of him, and he gasped, trying to catch his breath. Tyne crawled over to him. He patted Ward's sweat-soaked back. "You shouldn't have tried it," he said. "You just shouldn't have tried it."

Ward sat up. "Everyone get back?" he asked. He took a deep breath and looked around him.

"They got Tinker," Tyne said. "And I think they got Rankin. Rankin didn't come back."

"I thought there was only three," Ward said. "Jesus, is that Tinker?" He was looking at the hand that appeared over the wall.

Tyne nodded.

"Why don't you pull him in?"

"What's the use? He's dead."

"How do you know he's dead?"

"I can tell when a man's dead."

"Oh, hell," Ward said. "What a god-damned mess. What a bloody, god-damned mess."

"It could have been worse. They could have waited until you were all up there and then let you have it. It could have been a hell of a lot worse."

"It's bad enough," said Ward.

Tyne looked at Cousins and Tranella. "You all right?"

164

"In the pink," Tranella said. Cousins nodded.

"Tough luck," Tyne said. He turned back to Ward. "Now we've really got a job on our hands."

"Yeah," Ward said.

"There's no element of surprise, and they've got us cold. They know where we are and where we want to get to, and they probably know every way we'll use to try and get where we want to go. They've probably got a machine-gun in every window of that house. No one could get near enough to use a grenade."

"I wish to Christ we had a mortar," Ward said.

"It never happens the way you want it to happen," said Tyne. "If we had a mortar there'd be nothing to it."

"But we haven't got a mortar."

"No."

"How about waiting till dark?"

"We can't wait till dark," Tyne said. "We've got to get in there and get in there fast. I wish to God I could make them think we've got a mortar."

"Yeah," Ward said. "But how?"

"Nothing we can do."

Rivera spat on the barrel of his gun. The spittle rolled down, sizzling. "I'm a marksman," he said. "A marksman first class."

"I wonder who they knocked off," Friedman said. "Too damn far away to see."

"I hope it's Ward," Rivera said. "Ward gives me a pain in the pratt. All the sergeants give me a pain in the pratt."

"Tyne's all right," Friedman said.

"Yeah, Tyne's all right. But he ain't a sergeant."

"He probably will be."

"Then he'll give me a pain in the pratt."

Friedman stared down along the wall. The figure lying against it puzzled him. Within him he had a desperate urge to know who it was. He liked some men in the platoon better than others; he didn't want the body to be that of someone he liked. As a matter of fact, he didn't want it to be the body of anyone he knew, anyone he had worked with. "He's a big guy, whoever he is," he said.

"There's somebody else out in the field," Rivera said noncommittally.

"I know it. Didn't see him get hit, though."

"Ah, it was beautiful. The way I messed up that house was beautiful. I could do that fifty times a day."

"You'd better keep your eyes open," Friedman said, "or they'll be sending a halfback around this end with a grenade stuck in his mitt. They'll only have to do that once a day."

"The hell with it," said Rivera. "I've seen them coming around my end by the millions. They never gained a yard around my end. I'm indestructible. No-body dies."

"Okay, corpse," said Private Friedman.

It was up to Tyne. Responsibility weighed on his shoulders and creased his forehead. Cautiously he raised his head over the wall, behind Tinker's hand. The farmhouse was quiet again. It might have been a farm on a normal busy day, with all the men out in fields and all the women in the kitchen. It did not look like a theater of war. It seemed quiet, peaceful. It reminded Tyne vaguely of pictures he had seen on calendars in garages and grocery stores. You could sit in that place on the side of the road and be a friend to man.

*T-z-i-n-g-g-g.* He hit the ground as a bullet ricocheted from the wall and went whizzing off in the woods. "Close," he said. "Somebody up there's careless with firearms." Cousins grinned appreciatively, and Tyne felt better. The joke was an old one, but he supposed it was what he should say under the circumstances.

"They've got us cold," he said to Ward. "Pretty and cold."

"It's no place for a gentleman," Tranella said. He held up one hand. "Please, teacher, can I leave the room?"

"You and Tinker," Ward said. Tranella's hand came suddenly down, and he swallowed.

"We should have given you some cover too," Tyne said.

Ward shrugged. "What the hell, it wouldn't have made any difference. All I hope is they haven't put through a call to send a couple of tanks. That would really screw us."

The thought of tanks chilled Tyne. He caught himself. "I don't think they will," he said. "We've got a lot of planes around here. They're probably afraid the planes would see the tanks."

"What makes you think so?" Ward asked.

"I just got a feeling."

"I just got a feeling, too," Ward admitted. "I wonder if Rankin's dead."

For a moment Tyne had forgotten Rankin. Now he found himself remembering him with some embarrassment. "God, I don't know," he said.

"He's safe where he is, I guess. He can hang on."

"Yeah, if anyone can hang on Rankin can hang on."

Privates Carraway and James were lying on their stomachs, talking about nature. Private James had a leaf in his hand. They had developed, over a period of months, a core of hardness to anything that might happen. Already they had forgotten Rankin and Tinker. It was as though they had never existed. "Now take this leaf," Private James said. "Look at the complications. Think of all the trouble it took to make this leaf. You never saw nothing as complicated as that."

"I'm as complicated as that," said Private Carraway. "The human body is the god-damned most complicated thing in the world."

"It ain't no more complicated than this leaf."

"Ah, sure it is. That leaf's just a little thing. The human body's a lot bigger."

"That's what I mean," said Private James. "It's got a lot more to be complicated about. This leaf ain't got anything to be complicated about when you come right down to it."

"What's so fancy about it?"

"Look at the veins, for instance."

"You mean to tell me that leaves' veins is more fancy than human veins?"

"I didn't say that. I only said look at them."

"All right," Carraway said. "I'm looking at them. So what?"

"They're fancy."

"Ah, for Christ's sake," Carraway said. "I got no time for nature study. There's a war on."

"Never heard of it," said Private James innocently. But he threw his leaf away.

The map came out again, and again was spread on the ground. "The trouble with this map is that there's no detail about the farm," Tyne said. "It says the wall stops down by the river, but we knew that anyway. It doesn't show anything new at all. We might just as well toss it away."

Craven had crawled over to see what was going on. "How about the river?" he asked.

"What about it?" Tyne wanted to know. He ran his finger over the blue line on the map that marked it off, as though by the mere pressure of the flesh it could actually become water.

"Maybe we can circle the farm by the river," Craven said. "We can crawl along the bank."

The map once more became the object of study. How dead the symbols are! Tyne thought. They are meaningless, like flies crawling on a wall. He looked at the little black rectangles that signified the farm buildings, then at the elliptical lines that stood for the wall. They were cold and empty. "The only thing is," he said, "we don't know what they've got on that side of the farm."

"There's one way to find out," Ward said.

"What's that?"

"Send a patrol."

Tyne shook his head violently. "No," he said. "There isn't time any more. We've got to get in there, that's all."

"How about forgetting the farm entirely?" Craven said. "How about just crawling down the wall, then wading along this bank of the river until we get to the bridge and then blow her?"

It sounded good. "Idea," Ward said. Tyne stared at the map without speaking. He was looking at the location of the bridge. Whether it had been blown or not would make little difference to its position. If it had been blown the Germans would have put up some sort of pontoon affair right beside the old one, so that they could run back on to the road again. It looked as though there might be a bit of rock between the farm and the bridge; there was just a chance that it couldn't be seen from the windows. And there was also the chance that the Germans had no defences around the bridge. Perhaps they thought the farmhouse was enough protection. The Germans were so methodical that they always left something undone. They were too methodical. "It doesn't sound bad," he said.

"Hell, no," Ward said. "Best thing we can do."

"We've got to work fast," Tyne said. He looked at his watch. "Damned fast."

"Well, let's go," said Ward. "Best thing's a patrol. Four or five men."

Tyne was dubious. "I don't know," he said. "Perhaps there ought to be more. If there is anyone on the bridge four or five men can get tied up very nicely.

I'd rather send two big patrols. Say ten men in each. Send them one after the other. Then if the first one gets jammed up the second one can pitch in. That's the most logical thing."

"Whatever you want," Ward said.

Tyne folded the map very carefully. "The best thing would be a diversion. How long do you think it would take to get over around the farm, Ward?"

Ward thought for a moment. "Ought to allow about half an hour," he said. "Yeah, just about a half an hour."

"That's fast moving," Craven said.

"All right." Tyne nodded agreement. "What we'll do is this. Ward, you take one patrol and go first. Craven, you take the other one. I'll stay here with the rest of the platoon. We'll give you exactly a half an hour. Then we'll hop over the wall and head for the house. You'll know when we start, because I'll put Rivera to work. You can't help but know. The Krauts will think we're coming up on this side, and they'll pay us all the attention. Then you blow the bridge. As soon as we hear you blow it we'll all get up and rush the joint. How does that sound?"

Two vertical lines appeared at the bridge of Ward's nose. He was running the idea over in his head. "Yeah," he said finally. "It sounds right. How about you, Craven?"

"I don't know," Craven said. "I think they ought to start after twenty minutes. Then the Heinies might not pay so much attention to what's going on behind the house."

"You're right," Tyne said. "I never thought of it.

Well, that's the story, then. I guess it's about the best we can do."

"You've cut yourself out a tough job," said Ward.

"Suicide," Tyne said. "I'm a hero. We're all heroes. This'll mean the Good Conduct Medal."

"What the hell," Craven said. "It might be a breeze."

"It might be," said Tyne. "But I don't think so."

The men were lounging behind the wall, taking it easy. They didn't seem very much concerned about what was going to happen. Some of them were at their rations. A man can get hungry almost anywhere, under almost any circumstances. The stomach is a sensitive instrument, the seat of many things besides hunger, but it is still a very demanding instrument. Condemned men can eat a hearty breakfast, at least for the benefit of the yellow press. The soldier, who does not necessarily consider himself condemned to anything more than utter boredom, can eat a hearty meal at any time. The men were not even interested in Tinker's hand, poised above the wall. They had seen such things before. It was very much like going to a bad movie for the second time. It was wonderful what could bore them after a year of battle.

They thought of the farmhouse dispassionately. When Ward came among them, picking out his patrol, they were not moved one way or another. What they were about to do was merely a job, and they had probably been on worse jobs before. That, in itself, was one way to make things seem better. Cousins, for instance, swore that none of the action he had seen— and he had seen a great deal—had been comparable to the Louisiana maneuvers. The idea was to convince yourself that nothing that could come could possibly be as bad as what had gone before. You could last that way; you could last a long time that way. They went with Ward and they went with Craven, and the men who were to go with Tyne went to him calmly. It was the war. It was the job. It was *their* job. Get it done and then relax, that was the thing to do.

Tyne talked to them and they listened. The plan was simple, beautifully simple, the sort of simple thing that could easily go wrong. They listened carefully, nodding their heads occasionally, letting Tyne's words sink in. And when he was through they sat looking at him or studied their rifles or rubbed their hands slowly together as though the joints were aching.

# II

S OMEBODY'S COMING up here," Friedman said.

"Maybe it's Marlene Dietrich," Rivera said. "Has he got legs?"

"I can't see," Friedman said. "It's the way they walk in the Army. It's Joe Jack."

Private Jack came crawling toward them, sometimes rising to his feet and going into a crouching run. He often acted as company runner, and it was his proud boast that more bullets had missed him than anyone else in the Army. He had a charmed life, had Private Jack.

"Why the hell they always stick you out in left field?" he panted as he came up to the machine-gun. "Why don't you ever hang around where a guy can get at you?"

"There are three ways to do things," Rivera said solemnly. "The right way, the wrong way, and the Army way. It's the Army way to stick me out in left field. What you got, Joe?"

"Message from Tyne," Jack said. He passed over a folded paper.

Rivera opened it slowly. "Wish I had my glasses," he said.

"Cut it," Friedman said. "What's he say?"

" 'Doughfoot,' " Rivera read. " 'Two patrols going try go round farm via river. I taking rest platoon over field. When blow my whistle synchronize watch 1215 hrs. Five minutes after going up field on dot. Give cover 15 seconds before. Give cover up field. Remember, cover at 1219 and 45 secs. Hope ammo holds out. We are going all the way.' That's all."

"How's he sign it?" Friedman wanted to know.

"Tyne, Cpl., U.S.A.," said Rivera.

"Formal, ain't he?"

Rivera looked at his watch. "If this thing is right it's only two minutes to 1215. The patrols left, Joe?"

"Yeah, they left before I came here."

"Okay, hop back and say we're all set. Tell Tyne I said good luck."

"I'll tell him, Rivera." Jack turned and started back in his crouching run. Rivera looked carefully at the dial of his watch. "Nobody dies," he said. "How's the ammo?"

"It's been worse," Friedman said. "And it's been better."

"Tyne really cut himself a piece of cake," Rivera said. He studied the note. "Hey, Friedman, what's this mean? 'Five minutes after going up field on dot.' I don't get it."

"Let's see the note," Friedman said. He took it and peered closely at it. He read it over several times. "Oh, I get it," he said. "He means that five minutes after he blows his whistle they're going up the field. He wants you to go to work fifteen seconds before."

"That it?" Rivera took the note back. "Suppose they'll give me money for overtime?"

"Ah, sure," said Friedman.

"Jesus," Rivera said, "that's a tricky business."

Friedman looked glum. "Looks like we'll be getting a new platoon pretty soon."

"Yeah," Rivera said. Then suddenly the mask of lightness dropped from his face. He looked worn and angry and his dark eyes flashed. "God damn it," he burst out, "why don't they ever give them a chance? They never get a chance. We're the dirty god-damned Infantry and they stick us in everywhere. Jesus, there's a hell of a lot of good men going down in this war. Why don't they let us alone? I wish to God that I had every Nazi right in the palm of my hand. I'd crush them to a pulp. Why the hell don't they let us alone?" He subsided as quickly as he had begun.

"Yeah," Friedman said.

Rivera looked at his watch again. "It won't be long now," he said. "A whole new god-damned platoon."

Tyne watched the patrols go, wiggling along by the wall, their backs turned toward him. He wondered vaguely how many of the faces he would ever see again. Then he shook himself. That was the wrong kind of idea to have. It was just a job, that was all, just a job. Like any other job. It wasn't any more risky than working in a steel mill—not even as risky, perhaps. It was all in the point of view. The twenty-five men who were to go up the field with him were spread up and down the wall, three yards apart. Their faces, or those of their faces that he could see, looked set and tired. He glanced at his watch. Two minutes to go till 1215. He looked up to see if he could see Jack. There was no sign of him. Behind his head, with a foot of wall between them, Tinker's hand reared limply toward the sky. Tyne was vaguely conscious of it, as though it were trying to touch his back.

Ward had gone off almost carelessly. So had they all. That was the only way to go, as though one would be back in a few minutes, as though one were just running down to the corner for a paper or to make a phone call. When it was done that way it was easy. And it was always done that way; the dragged-out good-bys were always reserved for the movies. Tyne knew, however, that Ward did not expect him to get across the field. Ward thought he was throwing himself away. They had argued about it, not in so many words. Ward had said he thought the two patrols would be enough, without any diversion. Craven had thought the same thing. But Tyne was in command of the platoon. He thought a diversion was needed, and a diversion there would be. He was not afraid. He was not even worried. Everything, he kept telling himself, was going to be all right. Everything was going to be just lovely.

Silently Ward slid into the river. Now that he was down there things looked better than he had hoped they would. There was a solid screen of reeds and bushes between them and the farmhouse. It looked clear ahead. The river was not more than seventy-five feet across, but it was deep. Even by the bank he went in to his ribs. But as set-ups went, it didn't look too bad. Tranella splashed down behind him. Ward whirled around. "Take it easy, for God's sake," he whispered.

"Sorry, Sarge," Tranella said. "Slipped."

"Well, don't slip again."

The patrol moved forward through the water. Ward carried no rifle. He had a .45 in his left hand and a grenade in his right. Only three men in each patrol carried rifles. They were more in the way than anything else.

Behind Ward's patrol Craven entered the water, catching his breath as he did so. He was still trying to write that letter, but it kept taking curious twists in his mind. Right now it read: "Dear Frances, I am just back from going swimming in a river somewhere in Italy and we have just blown up the bridge so that anybody who tries to cross the river will have to go swimming, too." He was composing the letter subconsciously. Perhaps he ought to write one for Tinker, too. Tinker had been interested. "Dear Mom, I am now sleeping against a wall Somewhere in Italy. It isn't very comfortable but a man has to lie where he can these days. If you ever get to Italy you must come and see me for I am always going to be here." He caught at a bush to steady himself as his foot stepped on an object under the water. Then, steadied, he waded on. The water was strangely cold for such a hot day. Or perhaps it seemed cold because the day was so hot. Craven wasn't sure. It was hard to be sure of things.

Tyne saw Jack coming toward him, coming back from Rivera. He had made good time, but there wasn't a lot to spare. He looked at his watch. Forty seconds to go before he blew his whistle. The patrols had been out for fifteen minutes.

"How'd it go?" he asked as Jack came up to him.

"Rivera says it's okay," Jack said. "He said good luck."

"Nice of him," Tyne said. He looked at his watch and put the whistle to his lips. Every other watch was synchronized; only Rivera had to be checked. A few of the men were studying their own watches as though they expected to be surprised when Tyne blew his whistle. He puffed out his cheeks and let go.

"Right on the nose," Rivera said. "Even the lousy second hand was right on the nose."

"That's not an Army watch," Friedman said. "What kind of a watch is that?"

"Just a watch," Rivera said. "It works."

"I'm slow."

"How much time is it now? Oh, yeah, four minutes, forty-five seconds. Honest to God, I'm going to cut that house right in two."

"If the ammo holds out," Friedman said.

"The ammo had better hold out," Rivera said grimly.

On the river the two patrols heard Tyne's whistle sound, faint and far away. Ward looked at his watch. Tyne was right on time. That meant five minutes before the diversion. He calculated that they were already behind the farm. There was a bend in the river less than fifty yards away, and from the bend they would be able to see the bridge. The river, he noted, curved almost entirely around the farm. Everywhere there was silence. They made surprisingly little noise as they moved ahead; much less noise, as a matter of fact, than Ward had expected. That was good. So far things had been successful. With just a little bit of luck they might stay that way. Ward was beginning to believe that the Germans had been so interested in the farmhouse that they had entirely forgotten to watch the river or the bridge. That was what they got for being so interested in windows.

For another thing, he did not believe that German fire covered every field of view from the house. He had a feeling that there were rocks up ahead, between the house and the river, and that it would have been impossible for them to cover anything in that direction. Time would show soon enough whether or not he was right. Ward wondered if he could pull the pin out of a grenade with his teeth. He had never done it before.

"How do you feel about things, Arch?" Tyne said to Archimbeau.

They were sitting three yards from each other. Archimbeau was chewing moodily on a straw he had picked up.

"It's a long war," Archimbeau said. "That's all I know about it."

"Still worried about Tibet?"

"Sometimes I think we'll never get out of the Army. Honest to God, that's what I think."

"I used to think I'd never get in it. So I figure I'll get out of it some day. It could be worse."

"I don't know how," Archimbeau said. "You don't know. You don't get all the stinking details."

"I've got a stinking detail right now," Tyne said.

"Who hasn't? But what the hell. Maybe we can sleep all day tomorrow. Maybe Germany'll surrender tomorrow. Who knows?"

"Who knows?" Tyne said. He crouched and moved up along the wall, checking the men over, asking them if things were okay, making sure that everything was going to run smoothly. "Remember," he told each one of them, "when you hear the bridge blow, get up and run like hell for the farm." That was very important. When the Germans heard the bridge go they were going to be a very surprised group of young men, and it was necessary to take advantage of that surprise. If that went well, it was half the job. They all seemed to know that.

Tyne spoke to every man of the twenty-five. As he came back to his position beside Archimbeau his stomach was screwed up in a tight knot. He felt slightly ill and slightly dizzy. It was rather hard to breathe. He knew that they were all going through the same symptoms. It was the natural thing; it was expected.

He looked at his watch. 1219. Forty-five seconds to go, forty-five seconds before Rivera opened up. He crouched on one knee, facing the wall. Men on either side of him were doing the same thing. He had a sudden urge to write a letter, but he didn't know to whom he wanted to write. Desperately he wanted to put words on paper, but for the life of him he couldn't think of a recipient. There were so many people he would have liked to write to. Words welled up inside him. The desire to write was superseded by a desire to talk to somebody. He looked casually at Archimbeau and winked. Archimbeau winked back, his mouth twitching as he did so. Fifteen seconds to go.

The sun burned down with a radiance fiercer than ever before. It was as though someone had flipped a switch and turned it on full power. It was a most peculiar sensation, to feel the sun grow suddenly hotter. Tyne wondered if anyone else had noticed the phenomenon. He was on the point of asking Archimbeau if he had noticed it when Rivera's gun suddenly started firing.

It chattered off on the left like a riveting machine. It sounded like the pneumatic drills Tyne had heard countless times in countless streets. And as it chattered on, the German machine-gun began to fire, too. Good. They were looking for Rivera. That would give them time to get over the wall.

Ward heard the machine-gun and jerked his head up. They were just rounding the bend, moving very carefully. Before him he could see the bridge, a pontoon affair with about six or seven floats under it. There was no one around. They were going to get it sure as hell. Ward grinned to himself. His finger tightened around his grenade. He began to move a little faster through the water.

"Fifteen," Tyne said aloud. He stood bolt upright, blew his whistle, and leaped over the wall. Three men came over after him. As he went over the wall one of his outstretched feet struck Tinker's body, and the body collapsed on the earth. Tyne hit the dirt and dug his nose in, listening. The German machine-gun had switched in his direction. It was traversing the wall. Bullets cut into the stone over his head and then passed on.

The German machine-gun went silent. Either Rivera had hit it or they were changing belts. Two or three scattered rifles fired from the farm. Cautiously Tyne began to worm his way forward, over the same ground that Ward's patrol had covered a short while before. Through the grass he could see Archimbeau working ahead. Archimbeau had perhaps two yards' lead on him. He must have given a devil of a jump over the wall.

"Damned thing's stopped," Friedman yelled.

Rivera suddenly stopped firing. "I put enough goddamned lead in that thing to sink it," he said. "No wonder it stopped."

"They didn't find Baby," Friedman said.

"Nope," said Rivera. "They didn't find Baby." He opened fire again.

It was hard for a man to think as he crawled over the earth. All Tyne's thoughts were strangely disconnected. The farm seemed very far away. The work at hand no longer pressed on his mind. All that was automatic. What did bother him, though, was the fleeting ideas that flashed through his brain and then vanished. He found himself reviewing the whole day in snatches. He saw Porter's face, twisted, and Hoskins's face, set. He saw Trasker with his jaw gone and Mc-Williams with his hands stretched out as though they would protect him from the plane. It seemed to him that McWilliams had been dead a very long time—that he had been dead for an eternity and that for eternity he was doomed to go through that same impotent action of stretching out his arms. Sometimes Tyne could not distinguish the living from the dead. Faces had a tendency to run together, to blur, to become indistinct. They became as confused and as difficult to explain as the battles they had been in. They ran together like letters of ink in the rain. They had no real identity. They were swallowed up in a mist, in a vapor.

And so were Tyne's thoughts. One moment he saw himself sitting by the fire at home; the next moment he saw himself, as though from a great distance, crawling over a muddy plain. He did not recognize the landscape as a real one. He had never fought in such a place. But the landscape was familiar for all that. It was the landscape of dream. He had been moving through it for years; he would probably never find his way out of it.

The German machine-gun started up again. It was firing into the grass ahead of them now. Either the gunners were bad or they were taking their time, playing with them. Tyne looked at Archimbeau again. He was creeping doggedly ahead, his eyes fixed before him, his mouth slightly open. Tyne wondered if he were breathing through his mouth, and then he realized that he himself was. Silly. He crawled on.

The patrols were nearly at the bridge. It was deserted, absolutely deserted. Ward felt a glow creeping over him, engendered by the approaching destruction. There was something fine about destruction; it released something in him. Perhaps it was because, as a farmer, he had spent most of his life cultivating things, building them up. It was the attraction of opposites, an outlet for several kinds of energy. He looked forward with great glee to using his grenade. The mission was so easy that it was almost laughable. Ward had an urge to burst out in guffaws. It was all so god-damned funny. They were going to blow up a nice German bridge. It was like little boys on Hallowe'en, stealing the parson's gate. Just like Hallowe'en.

"Damned foolish thing to do," Tyne said aloud. But he didn't know what was foolish or why he said it. He looked back at the wall and judged from his position that they were almost where Ward had been earlier. They still had a long way to go, a hell of a long way. Nothing was slower than crawling, nothing in the world. How long would it take to crawl around the earth? A hundred years? A thousand years? He ducked as the machine-gun spat over his head. He almost asked himself why they didn't depress the gun a little. It would be so easy.

Ahead of him he caught sight of a body, dark against the brown grass. He thought that he had been crawling where someone had been before, but he hadn't been sure; a cow might have come through the field. The body must be Rankin. He was possessed of an intense desire to know whether or not Rankin was still alive. He very nearly rose to his feet in his haste to get to the body.

Rankin was lying face down. With an effort Tyne managed to roll him over, but even as he rolled him he knew that he was dead. A dead body is completely devoid of any buoyancy. It is a mere lump. Rankin had a hole in his neck and a hole in his chest, and he had holes in his back, also, where the bullets had entered in. His tommy-gun lay beside him. Tyne cast an anxious glance at Archimbeau, to see that he didn't get too far ahead of him, and picked up the tommy-gun. There was blood on it, covering the notches that marked Rankin's kills. Tyne laid his own rifle down beside Rankin and started crawling again. He took the tommy-gun with him.

How were they making out—all the faces, all the bodies? How were Cousins and Jack and MacNamara and Peterson and all the rest of them? Did they feel the way he did? Were they thinking the way he was thinking? They had come a long way to the war, and it would be a long way back. Over their heads and before their eyes the machine-gun sent its bullets in their vicious arc. It was death, alive and spitting. For all Tyne knew, some of the men had been hit already. There was no way of knowing. No way at all. Pictures flashed across his mind and were gone before he could grasp them. Everything speeded up; the world was moving at a dizzy pace. He could not keep up with it. It was going around faster and faster. In a minute it would fly away.

A dull explosion came from behind the farm. Then another and another. The bridge. Ward.